HAUNTED
SAVANNAH

SECOND EDITION

HAUNTED SAVANNAH

MACABRE MANSIONS, SOUTHERN SPIRITS, AND BONE-CHILLING BURIAL GROUNDS

GEORGIA BYRD

Globe
Pequot

ESSEX, CONNECTICUT

Globe Pequot

An imprint of Globe Pequot, the trade division of
The Rowman & Littlefield Publishing Group, Inc.
4501 Forbes Blvd., Ste. 200
Lanham, MD 20706
www.rowman.com

Distributed by NATIONAL BOOK NETWORK

British Library Cataloguing in Publication Information available

Library of Congress Cataloging-in-Publication Data
Names: Byrd, Georgia R., author.
Title: Haunted Savannah : macabre mansions, Southern spirits, and bone-chilling
    burial grounds / Georgia Byrd.
Description: Second edition. | Essex, Connecticut : Globe Pequot, [2023] | Series:
    Haunted | Includes bibliographical references.
Identifiers: LCCN 2022060032 (print) | LCCN 2022060033 (ebook) | ISBN
    9781493070367 (paperback) | ISBN 9781493070374 (ebook)
Subjects: LCSH: Ghosts—Georgia--Savannah. | Haunted places—Georgia—
    Savannah.
Classification: LCC BF1472.U6 B97 2023 (print) | LCC BF1472.U6 (ebook) | DDC
    133.109758/1—dc23/eng/20230322
LC record available at https://lccn.loc.gov/2022060032
LC ebook record available at https://lccn.loc.gov/2022060033

To my husband, Joseph, who believed me when I said, "I just saw a ghost."

CONTENTS

ACKNOWLEDGMENTS

Special thanks go to my dear friends and Savannah colleagues who fed me some of the South's most intriguing tales. I must thank Gene Downs, one of the profession's greatest critics, who steered me in the direction of fiction. My new friends at the Georgia Historical Society have also been helpful. My faithful editor, Greta Schmitz at Globe Pequot Press, is to be commended for her constant encouragement and guidance. Also, special thanks to my son, Whit, who brought the fictional "Ghostbusters" to life every day of his childhood by wearing a one-piece jumpsuit and backpack, fighting off anything that his imagination could conjure. To this day, he continues to hang skeletons in the shower and jump out from around corners just to get a scream.

AUTHOR'S NOTE

These stories are retold fictionally based on Savannah tales and legends. In some instances, names have been changed. Some private homes are referenced, so heed Southern courtesy and respect the home owners' privacy as you explore the world beyond in the South's most intriguing city.

INTRODUCTION

"We fall from womb to tomb, from one blackness and toward another, remembering little of the one and knowing nothing of the other . . . except through faith."

—Stephen King, *Danse Macabre*

"This house is haunted," my fourteen-year-old son, Whit, said as we unpacked our car to move into a modest, ranch-style home on Wilmington Island, about eight miles east of Savannah's Historic District. I can't recall what I replied, but I'm sure it went something like this: "You're silly. There is no such thing as ghosts, and don't you believe any nonsense such as that."

We took possession of our home in 1998. Ironically, it was the afternoon of Halloween.

For the first few months, we encountered some strange, but nonthreatening, oddities. For example, as the family tuned into *Jeopardy* one evening, the doorbell rang, but there was no one on the porch when we answered it. Soon after, the annoying doorbell ringing became a nightly ritual. My crafty husband finally disconnected it. To our astonishment, it would still ring. And then there was the wine stain that wouldn't go away, even after repeated cleanings. There were nights when we joked about "the bloody spot where someone was murdered," amusing ourselves with theories that never made much sense.

Our final challenge came in September of 1999. That's when we all decided we'd had quite enough.

It was a little short of a year from the day we had moved in. News reports blasting a mandatory evacuation set the family in motion. Hurricane Floyd was projected to head up the eastern coast and straight to our city. We packed our most cherished items—the computer, family photos, and paintings—and loaded up my mother-in-law, son, and four dogs in two separate cars. We drove all night on a long, mountainous trek to our Aunt Lorene's vacation home in Brevard, North Carolina.

Eighteen hours and several traffic jams later, we unlocked the door to the cottage, starving and exhausted from the intensity of the drive. As we walked into the kitchen, we were startled by a dated, corn-yellow dial phone on the cypress kitchen wall that seemed to be ringing off its mount. My body stiffened in shock, and I felt a rush of blood flow from my face down to the tips of my fingers when I answered it and recognized the voice of one of our Savannah neighbors.

"You know that skylight you've always wanted?" he asked. "Well, you've got it now. The hurricane and possibly a small tornado just ripped through your house, leaving it exposed to the elements, and most of your belongings are floating in standing water."

On our way back home the next morning, we stopped at a convenience store to refuel and purchased an *Augusta Chronicle* newspaper. Shockingly, there was our Savannah home on the front page! The photo showed a structure completely cut in two by a giant pine tree. What it didn't show was the mess inside. The ceiling was on the floor. Picture frames were shattered and lying in pieces on the molding furniture. The hot water heater in the attic was dangling over the living room couch through a wide gash that opened up to the sky. By the time we arrived home, water was standing in the house and it was starting to fill with mosquitoes and mold.

By this time, we were certain: Someone or something was trying to keep our family from getting too comfortable in this house.

Our insurance agent met us in the front yard and made a startling announcement: "Your house was the only home in Savannah to receive damage from the storm."

We moved out and into an apartment, where we enjoyed a normal existence for six months. Finally, when inspections on our house were complete, we moved back into a home that rivaled a newly constructed dwelling. We were starting fresh with an attractive new roof, solid white doors, decorative furnishings, modern fixtures, and shimmering hardwood floors.

But evil would not sleep.

I was busy writing in my newly renovated office just off the garage. Our Jack Russell terrier, Snorkel, was at my feet chasing squirrels in her dreams. As I worked, I detected an unnerving sound like that of sandpaper grating across an old piece of furniture. I looked down to see if Snorkel had nabbed a rogue lizard or was digging in the mounds of paper and magazines I stored beneath my desk. She was sound asleep.

After another five minutes, I spun my chair around and saw a pair of gravel-colored snakes about four inches in diameter and at least five feet long inter-twined and slithering in a vertical direction. They appeared to be in a locked position, which put me in a sheer panic. To make matters worse, I was going to have to pick up the dog and pass within two feet of the reptiles to get out the door.

Shaking like fall leaves on a windy day, I dashed out the door with the dog cradled in my arms like a baby. Once I was in the garage and sheltered from the terror, I let my screams echo throughout the neighborhood. Suddenly, the words of my son came to mind: "This house is haunted."

My mind went back to closing day in the lawyer's office with the former own-ers. They had lived in the house for less than a year before abruptly putting it on the market.

I shared my thoughts in confidence with a Christian friend and pastor's wife, who advised me to use the Bible to cast out the demons I believed were consuming my house. "Good always overcomes evil," she said. Because I was embarrassed to share this upcoming ritual with my family for fear they might think I was mad, she and I went about our mission within a week of the snake ordeal.

We entered each room of the house, both of us grasping the word of God and holding it high while declaring our faith. We completed our voodoo-like ceremony with haste and, afterward, chatted incessantly over coffee about unrelated things in perfect peace, as if nothing had ever happened.

Today, there's a Bible in every room and two or three in some. And since that day, we've enjoyed a normal existence, free of Satan's terrifying antics.

Much like our home, Savannah is teeming with tales of the supernatural. The occurrences in private homes, inns, and other historic buildings are so frequent and ongoing, it is difficult to narrow them down in one sitting. Ghost Hunters (from the syndicated TV show), Ghost Chasers of America (a club), psychics, and even private citizens have devoted time and money to searching for meaning behind the haunts in this city. At times witches and even educated parapsychologists with sophisticated equipment have investigated to no avail.

For, you see, this city has been declared one of the "most haunted in the United States" on more than one occasion, both in print and on television. What makes the old port city so haunted? Why are spirits constantly showing their wits in both good and evil ways here?

There is, in reality, no logical answer, but many have made educated guesses. Savannah was established in 1733, and her history is full of intriguing characters who lived and died through various fortunes and misfortunes. With the downtown area hailed as one of the nation's largest National Historic Districts, many of Savannah's magnificent homes have been restored, and a number of them reflect the traditions, the decor, and in many cases the original furnishings of former inhabitants. Within the walls of many of these structures are hidden passageways, dungeons, and an abundance of shocking ordeals and family tragedies. Cemeteries once located in central parts of town were moved and bodies relocated (as others were left behind) to other burial sites through the years. In the 1700s and 1800s, early settlers fought both natural disasters ranging from intense storms to floods, fires, and disease. In 1796 when a stove fell, a fire began and spread across several blocks. The fire destroyed three hundred buildings and consumed several homes and their inhabitants. According to historic records, a fire in January 1820 began in a boardinghouse and destroyed an estimated $4 million in buildings from Broughton Street to the Savannah River. Many perished.

Those fires were fueled by strong winds that ravaged the city and gunpowder that was stored in Ellis Square. Many downtown buildings and homes were destroyed.

In 1820, the yellow fever virus claimed the lives of nearly seven hundred residents. That same year, poor sanitary conditions proved ideal for mosquito breeding, and epidemics of malaria broke out along the flourishing Georgia coast. To further substantiate the many alleged supernatural sightings, some victims of the disease were erroneously proclaimed dead and may have been buried alive.

In 1864, federal troops assisted in dousing an explosive fire that began in an ammunition depot on Broughton Street. More than a hundred buildings were lost, and many of those inside also died. In 1889, fifty buildings burned and troops from Charleston, Atlanta, Jacksonville, and Macon were called in to assist, to no avail.

By far the worst disaster to strike Savannah occurred from 1824 through 1854, when yellow fever spread through the city, afflicting citizens of all ages with severe fever, backaches, vomiting, and hemorrhaging. As Savannahians appealed to physicians for answers, the disease continued to kill with a vengeance. Officials at the city's only medical facility, Candler Hospital (then located on East Huntingdon Street), began to hide the dead in an underground morgue to keep the numbers a secret and to discourage panic. By the time they learned that mosquitoes were the cause of the disease, hundreds had perished. Perhaps some of the spirits who wander the streets today are products of the epidemic.

The 1800s brought the first in a series of hurricanes to Savannah. Several passed either east or made direct landfall, but one of the more forceful storms passed directly over Tybee Island and caused extensive damage and flooding on the island and in downtown Savannah. As a result, graves were exposed and some even opened. Spiritual beings refusing to sleep eternally now coexist with Savannahians and the city's visitors. Nearly every day, tales of unnerving experiences arise. From historic downtown structures to modern apartment complexes on the islands to creepy venues at the beach, these spirits haunt and taunt, yearning for everlasting rest that will not come. They appear when least expected and vanish in a breath.

Many who died have unsettled business keeping them from the peace of heaven or the wrath of hell. They are not all evil, and some are even comical, or at least entertaining, but the thread of achieving finality in this life has not yet been woven into their existence.

So as you read this book, don't let creaky floors, cold spots, disappearing apparitions, and moving objects lead you astray. There's more to this haunted locale than mere tales. Savannah is a city replete with a naturally creepy ambience. Her aesthetics exude fear. Embraced by oaks that never turn brown (called live oaks due to their "evergreen" status), Savannah is shaded by massive branches that spread and reach out, often connecting like arthritic hands linked together. The trees cast a constant shroud of shade over the parks and squares and mansions like a backdrop of special effects woven into a creepy movie trailer. Those backdrops are accentuated by mysterious forms of the moss that hangs like graying, shaggy beards and inexplicably thrives in humidity. The results are reflected in this historic city's revolving stage. Hence, Savannah's showcase of horror is critically acclaimed for fulfilling her terrifying reputation.

It is, therefore, my duty to prompt chills and keep you up at night as you read these frightening tales. I've mixed the gruesome stories with theatrics in order to retell the terrifying realities that touch the lives of Savannahians to this day. It is difficult to prove beyond a shadow of a doubt the absolute worth of these accounts, so don't even try. Decide for yourself whether or not you are a believer. As for me, I need no convincing.

NO REST FOR SARAH

Visitors from all over the world travel en masse to walk the hallways of the stately mansion that was the childhood home of Savannah's most famous nineteenth-century lady, Juliette Gordon Low. Revered as the founder of the Girl Scouts, her home at the corner of Oglethorpe and Bull Streets is one of Savannah's most prominent houses. It is also one of the city's most haunted.

The proclamation was definitive.

If we were going to conduct an interview about whether spirits dwell in the stately mansion at the northeast corner of Oglethorpe and Bull Streets, the ground rules must first be declared.

Sitting in a stiff wooden chair in the administrative office and discussing ghosts was a little unnerving, to say the least. Although the room resembled an office, a defiant being was telling us that it was once a bedroom, and perhaps a bedroom where death had overcome life. We were sensitive to the room's history with each passing moment, and yet we were also engulfed by the eerie presence of another being.

As Linda, the museum's director, and I spoke, we were cautiously choosing our words as if someone were eavesdropping on our chat.

"First off, I want you to know that we love our ghosts. They are endearing. We accept them. They are a part of our family."

I assumed that her words were a declaration of sorts, pledging all respect to a ghost who was sitting in on our meeting, somewhere in this room, perhaps with legs crossed.

Linda was intent on whispering. While she spoke, my hands were clenched tightly underneath the thick oak table.

"OK, understood."

"Next, these are friendly spirits. They are stuck here. We don't know why. They just are." She looked around as though she was checking to see if anyone else would respond to her bold statements.

"OK, understood."

As the minutes ticked away on the wall clock behind us, she continued to speak in a strange, cautious manner, as though she were choosing her words to deliberately shed honor on the spirits. Her voice resonated with a quiver as her fluttering hands reached out to hand me a stack of historic documents.

The Gordon family history in the majestic nineteenth-century dwelling was indeed spellbinding. I began to peruse the documents as Linda highlighted some of the family's more colorful characters.

One story caught my eye, and I suddenly (and rudely) tuned out my hostess. The Gordon family history was filled with all the elements of life, death, and tragedy, and an unsettling atmosphere was filling the room as we continued. I was intrigued by the tragic story of a woman who had given birth to twins, both stillborn, in a second-floor bedroom. There was a marriage built on abuse that ended in divorce, and there was a tender love story about a husband who died before his time, laced with a tale of the beautiful young daughter who died in her twenties of scarlet fever.

At first, I barely noticed the sensation of someone standing behind me and looking over my shoulder. Through my thoughts, I could distinctly hear a person breathing. Before I could change position, cold air struck the back of my neck in a distinct puff. I assumed that someone had walked in so quietly that, fascinated by the story of the ill-fated mother, I did not notice. I glanced up at Linda, expecting her to welcome the visitor, but she was engaged in making a list of my requested documents on a piece of paper.

As she wrote, I turned and found the room empty. A cold draft wafted through the third-floor office as if a window had been opened in the middle of winter. Both windows were closed—and the temperature outside was a very Savannah-steamy ninety degrees.

As the sudden burst of chill swallowed our words, an awkward silence left space for an even stranger occurrence. A computer printer sitting on a desk behind us suddenly lit up and began to hum as if it had been prompted to warm up for a job. No one was seated at the desk. There were no other computers tied into it.

The printer light turned green and chugged up again. This time, it didn't shut off.

I had been forewarned that the ghosts of the Juliette Gordon Low Birthplace enjoy disturbing office equipment, leaving the staff no choice but to unplug each and every item at the end of each day. Otherwise, either someone on the staff was a prankster, or I was hallucinating.

Downstairs, the day's first troop of Girl Scouts had arrived for their heralded mission to walk the hallways of their founder. We caught their giggles drifting upward from the ground floor. The Juliette Gordon Low Birthplace was coming alive on a typical summer morning. More than forty thousand girls visit each year, traveling in small, lively herds from all over the world to discover the inspiring stories that built the now famous Girl Scouts of the USA. They come to see the rooms where "Daisy," as she was called, spent her life as a small child, as a schoolgirl, as a debutante, as a young bride, and as a mature lady.

A few of the more astute Scouts were quick to admit that they had read about the mansion's hauntings. They had come to learn about their founder's life and, perhaps, see a ghost.

The presence of these girls lent an air of joyfulness in contrast to the formal and noble Regency-styled structure. Bearing toothy grins illuminated by gleaming braces, they were dressed in T-shirts and sashes emblazoned with troop names. Armed with backpacks, bottled water, and mobile phones, the girls and their leaders took turns snapping photos on the staircase in front of the home's distinguished entrance. It's a ritual that occurs most days of the year.

Ten-year-old Jennie, from Michigan, was among this day's tourists. Jennie and her troop had viewed the house from the sidewalk the previous evening. They had enjoyed a walking ghost tour of the city, and their guide told them all about the home's ghost, Nelly, whom he described as being "often seen through the window peering out to tourists on the streets." It was on that tour that Jennie flinched and stared at the elongated windows in the hopes of catching a glimpse of the paranormal. What she saw was a portion of the thickly lined draperies blowing from a kick of the room's air-conditioning vents.

On this morning, Jennie grasped her cell phone, which was already in camera mode, as they made their way into the house. After being hushed by her leader, she followed the guide through the rooms that she had read about online. She listened intently as the guide described the home's colorful history, while in the back of her mind all she could think about was the ghost she would see today.

With my hands nervously soaked (and still clenched) from the various thumps and bumps in the room, I began to gather my notes for the tour of the mansion. As Linda and I stood and turned toward the door, a loud knocking stopped us in our tracks.

Someone was violently shaking the French doors that led out into a small foyer. I glanced toward Linda for reassurance that didn't come.

A petite, elderly woman with strong hands was clutching the doorknobs, rattling the doors back and forth as if she were trying to get in. She was wearing period clothes: a mauve dress and a strange brooch at the neck.

Our screams escaped like those of a Halloween fright house. And then she vanished.

"That was Sarah."

"Oh."

Sarah had threatened our peace, and for some reason, she did not want me to tour the home. I needed no more convincing. It was official. The Juliette Gordon Low Birthplace was indeed haunted.

"Don't be afraid," Linda said. "Our ghosts are friendly."

She had already told me this just minutes before, and I was questioning her repeated statement as well as the words that I knew she wanted to say.

Linda led the way to the staircase and down, stopping along the way to describe life as it was in the 1800s. Traipsing down the stairs to the main level, we passed the Girl Scout troop from Michigan. Jennie was wide-eyed. Our eyes met and then drifted.

Jennie's troop followed behind, overwhelmed by the display of wealth of an old Savannah family. Their youthful minds captured the intricate architectural elements of plaster and wood motifs that adorned the ceilings. There were influences from all cultures, including Greek and Roman, with ceilings abloom with rosettes of bellflowers and acanthus leaves. Making our way into the main parlor, we glanced to the right, where an antique glass case bearing Gordon family relics stood.

There, in the hallway, hung a portrait of a woman—the woman we had just seen shaking the office doors.

Her mouth was turned down in a sad sort of way, and she was wearing a cap that crowned her coarse gray hair that was parted in the middle. Her eyebrows were dark and thick, like a man's. Her cape was drawn up at the neck and cinched with a brooch. Earlier, we passed another portrait of a younger Sarah. Her hair was dark and her mouth turned up at the corners in a happier and more relaxed smile. It was clear that tragedy had brought sadness upon her demeanor in the second portrait.

Our guide ushered us into the main parlor and toward the antique glass cupboard. Removing a brooch, she began to tell a tale of unbearable heartache and loss. Her story went like this:

Construction of the house began in 1818 and took three years to complete. Hoping to create a family home that was as distinguished as himself, Savannah mayor James Moore Wayne oversaw the customization of the interior to his liking, with plenty of receiving rooms for socializing and spacious living quarters on the second floor and above. There were four bedrooms with dressing rooms, a hall, and possibly two small bedroom passages. Servants were housed in the attic and basement.

In 1831, Wayne sold the home to his great-niece Sarah Anderson Stites Gordon and her husband, William Washington Gordon I. Gordon became the first Georgian ever to graduate from West Point and was a founder of the Central of Georgia Railroad—he was a man who was highly respected both civically and professionally. With an extravagant new home set in the beautiful downtown area of Savannah, the Gordons planned to enjoy an active social life as they raised their seven children. But all did not go well for Sarah and her husband.

Two children, both boys, had died in childbirth. Their daughter Alice contracted scarlet fever and passed away suddenly when the physicians could not save her. Tragedy struck again in 1842, when at the age of forty-six, William, Sarah's beloved husband, died of complications from malaria while working on the construction of the Central of Georgia Railroad. Upon his death, Sarah was instructed by her husband's will to relocate the family to New Jersey to be near his relatives, who could assist her in fulfilling the children's education needs. Although it meant leaving her beautiful home and sacrificing the mild Savannah winters for cold northeastern ones, Sarah was obedient to her husband's request. She packed up the children and headed north.

William, she said, believed that education was better in the Northeast and it would be best for his children to attend school there. Willed to the estate, the house was closed and sat completely empty for ten years.

With Sarah receiving only a small stipend and the Savannah residence held in trust, the struggling widow accepted the challenges of raising her remaining children in New Jersey on a meager income. In tribute to her husband, the Central of Georgia Railroad extended her free transportation for the rest of her life.

Sarah's love for her home left in Savannah would remain strong in her heart, a heart that was broken not only by the passing of her beloved husband, but also for having to abandon the residence that she and her family adored.

Her immeasurable affection toward her deceased husband became more evident with each passing day following his death, and she dreamt of fitting tributes to honor him. One evening, she grasped the handrail of the stairs, climbed them slowly, entered her bedroom, and opened a dresser drawer. Inside the drawer with her floral-scented perfumes and gold-plated combs, she grabbed a pair of sharp scissors and proceeded to cut off a lock of her thick gray hair.

Opening the drawer below, she removed a tiny box with her husband's engraved initials. Inside were strands of his graying hair, which she had cut from his cold body as it rested in an ornate casket. On a night when her grief had escalated into long, heaving sobs, Sarah took his locks and created a tiny braid with her own hair. As a personal tribute to their love, she commissioned a jeweler to design a pair of rectangular-shaped gold brooches, each of which contained a thin braided strand of her husband's hair placed next to a braid of hers.

With William's estate divided among the children, times were difficult for Sarah, the widow who had now seen her children through to adulthood. Her son "Willie" Gordon, a Yale graduate, married Eleanor "Nelly" Kinzie of Chicago (the mother of Juliette, who was called Daisy), and the couple moved into the Wayne-Gordon House to live with their mother, who by this time was elderly. When Sarah became ill, she was sent back to New Jersey, where she died in 1882. It is said that she mourned the passing of her husband with intense grief all the remaining days of her life.

In short, nothing ever went Sarah's way. Three of her children had died—two sons in childbirth and a daughter—in addition to a daughter-in-law. Her husband's life had been cut short, and she found herself a widow well before her time. There would be no rest for her grieving spirit.

As the guide wrapped up her presentation, it became clear that, contrary to what the ghost tour guide had presented the night before, it was Sarah who had been haunting the Juliette Gordon Low Birthplace, not Nelly.

This was a place that employees and hundreds of happy girls fill with laughter and love, yet a subliminal cloud of grief hangs like the Spanish moss over Savannah oaks, consuming the joy. That grief that was once thought of as Nelly's, now, it seems, comes from Sarah.

Sarah is a busy ghost. She tidies up when the house is empty. She moves relics and hides collectibles. She plays with office equipment and turns computers on and off. She attends funerals. She peeks out of windows when no one is in the house, scaring visitors as she chuckles and shakes the draperies. At times she waltzes through the house and vanishes into its walls. She greets employees when they return to work, and she taunts them when they doubt her existence.

"We speak to Sarah on a daily basis," Linda said. "It's almost like she works here too. She's filled with mischief, and you'd better respect her. If you do or say something she doesn't like, she'll let you know in a big way."

My day was over. I thanked Linda for her time and exited the building.

Dashing past the ticking meters on Bull Street, racing to reach my car before the meter reader did, I suddenly came to a halt, realizing that I had left a binder full of notes upstairs in the third-floor office. I switched directions.

Entering the front hallway, I opened the door and rushed up the stairwell that by this time was empty. Suddenly, my steps were halted by her presence.

There Sarah stood, grimacing with arms folded. Her look was admonishing. Trying to speak, my efforts were fruitless. The words would not come.

Quickly she vanished, and my fear drove me straight out the front door, leaving all notes behind.

Back on the street, I glanced to see Jennie and her troop lined up for a picture in front of the home's grand exterior. Excited but disappointed at not having a ghostly encounter to share with her brothers back home, she handed her mobile phone over to their tour guide and the shutter clicked, capturing the perfect photo for her scrapbook: ten girls and their leader laughing on the steps of the Juliette Gordon Low Birthplace.

Jennie was going to hit SEND to text her mother the photo of her troop as they prepared to depart for the next Savannah landmark. But first, she opted to view the picture.

Behind her friends' smiling faces was a woman wearing period clothes and a brooch at her neck, peering through the draperies. She scrolled back to the photograph she had taken of the portrait of Sarah hanging in the home's hallway. As she studied that picture, she viewed the reflection of her own face in the portrait's glass. Flipping back and forth between the pictures, Jennie heard her friends calling her name.

"Hurry up! Stop playing with your phone. We're leaving you if you don't move along."

Why had Sarah revealed herself to Jennie and not the other girls? Why was Jennie's face showing in the portrait of Sarah hanging in the hallway?

Jennie hit SEND. She kept her thoughts to herself as she nervously placed the phone back into her pocket.

I rushed to my car, filled with thoughts of the story I was going to write without so much as a note to follow. As I dashed past the Girl Scouts, our eyes met, Jennie's and mine.

Nothing was said. We needed no words. We both knew that we had been touched by the ghost of Sarah.

WILLIE AND NELLY

Whose are the ghostly fingers that play so beautifully on the piano in the front parlor of the Juliette Gordon Low Birthplace? What possesses a woman to gleefully slide down the banister of a home so filled with love? Could there be other spirits, perhaps lovers who were separated by death but are now together again in the home they relished? This is the story of two lovers, Eleanor "Nelly" Kinzie Gordon (1835–1917), the mother of "Daisy" (the founder of the Girl Scouts), and her beloved husband, William "Willie" Washington Gordon II, who returned after his death on the day of hers to escort her to eternity.

The handcrafted musical instrument displayed in the Gordon family parlor was indeed a romantic heirloom—a classic zither—that held many memories, both sad and joyful. Margaret's eyes were drawn to its beauty the first time she visited the family mansion and saw it lying on the mahogany coffee table. The instrument, curved like the silhouette of a shapely woman on one side and straight like a door frame on the other, boasted the same rich colors as the table beneath it, blending in like an ornamental accent.

As far as she knew, the instrument—with its sensuous curves and mother-of-pearl inlay—had been there since the day the Gordons moved into the mansion. Closing her eyes, she recalled the stories of the many generations of Gordon women who had strummed and plucked the strings, at times sweetly singing songs of celebration or of grief, depending on the occasion.

Margaret's mother-in-law, Nelly, insisted that she learn to play it. Margaret had never questioned her motives, as she deeply longed for acceptance into the family. Without ever having studied music, she quickly learned to strum by ear, but lacking the motivation to expand her newfound talent, she had neglected to pick the instrument up again until the day Arthur brought it up to the bedroom of his dying mother.

"Play this for mother," he suggested, placing it in her open arms as she sat next to the bed.

By now it was clear.

"I learned to play for this day," Margaret murmured to herself. Gently strumming the harp-like instrument to the tune of a classic hymn, she felt as though the notes were somehow taking the pain away. As she played, she quietly sang the words:

When peace, like a river, attendeth my way,
When sorrows like sea billows roll,
Whatever my lot, Thou has taught me to say,
It is well, it is well, with my soul.

The gentle sounds of the hymn resounded with finality in the darkened room filled with a cloud of gloom.

As her pale fingers stroked the taut strings, Margaret could not help glancing tearfully at the dying woman who lay beneath a mound of coverlets.

"It's as if she were already dead," Margaret thought. "As if she were already dead and they have buried her here beneath billowing clouds." For some reason, this curious image calmed her, and she suddenly realized that she had been playing the same hymn continuously for several minutes.

A sense of overwhelming peace began to fill the room, and Margaret continued the conversation she was having with herself.

She hadn't looked forward to this task. Who would? After all, she wasn't related by blood. But her husband, Arthur, and his sisters begged for a break, so she volunteered. Little did she know that sitting in a stiff, cane-bottomed chair in the gloomy third-story room would drive her to pass the time with a musical instrument that she hadn't played in years. And little did she know that she would soon have an audience that would forever change her views of life after death.

It was a morbid charge for a dainty woman of the 1800s. But standing vigil over her mother-in-law's dwindling life was a proper gesture and a declaration of her love for her grieving husband. She would accept the challenge without complaints and sit patiently among the ornate furnishings: a thickly woven Oriental rug that felt good on her stocking-clad feet, and several wonderfully oversize heirlooms—a massive antique dresser, a splendid four-poster bed, and a tall grandfather clock with a powerful gong.

Adorned with fine linen blankets brought by train from New York, her mother-in-law lay clad in a thin white nightgown that was weighted down by several hand-crocheted blankets stacked beneath a thick, handmade quilt.

In spite of the ravaging disease, Nelly's emaciated face was angelic and peaceful, unlike her contagious character that fascinated most everyone she met. Prior to her illness, she was a boisterous, aggressive, and playful sort, and she was marked by those same traits until she fell ill on the eve of her last family gathering in the parlor of the mansion.

Yellow fever was spreading throughout Savannah, and Nelly had tried to stay away from those who were sick, as local physicians warned that the disease was contagious. Little did she know that when the elongated windows of her home were opened to let in the cool but humid summer breezes, the disease had crept in on the wings of a mosquito that landed on the silky, white skin of her forearm. It wouldn't take long for her to become another one of Savannah's victims.

There was hardly a breath left in her lungs as Margaret studied the gentle movements of Nelly's chest. Tenderly and on the verge of motionless, it raised up and down at an intensely labored pace. The strumming of the instrument soon became a monotonous distraction, so Margaret placed it beside the bed and continued her vigil in silence.

Then the rhythm of Nelly's breathing became rythmic with the sounds of the clock.

"Tick, breathe, tick, breathe, tick."

The stately grandfather clock stood in the corner as if it were keeping watch over the room and its inhabitants.

Margaret's mind raced back to the evening she first toured the grand old home that belonged to her husband's family. She had always admired that clock, and as she studied the family heirloom, it struck three times, igniting a startled blink in her tired blue eyes and causing her to jump.

A strong sigh cut through the silence. And then there was nothing.

Was this Nelly's last breath? Should she call out for Arthur and the others to come in for their last good-byes? How was she to know when God's final gift of breath would take the matriarch of this loving home to a casket awaiting her in the parlor, already crowded with loved ones?

Margaret stood up hastily and reached for the home's beautiful ceiling, stretching the stiffness out of a body that had been sitting in a hard chair for far too many hours. She would reconfirm the signs of life (or was it death?) first before fetching the doctor.

She peeled back the covers, exposing Nelly's stick-thin legs. Her plump and matronly figure had withered away to a skeletal state. Even the skin on her face was pulled taut to her forehead, revealing cheekbones that no one ever suspected she had.

Margaret felt Nelly's feet and took note that her body was beginning to stiffen while the warmth of her skin was turning to cold. Her lips were dried and her mouth was parched.

Should she swab her lips with water? Would that speed or slow the process? Or was she already gone?

"Arthur," she thought. "I will call for Arthur."

Nelly was growing weaker, and with each pant, her frail body cried out as if she were begging God for mercy to grant her only one more last agonizing breath.

And then she was gone.

Just as Margaret leaned down to kiss the solemn face of the departed woman, a voice called out to her.

"I beg your pardon, Madam! Please excuse yourself, for I have come to fetch my bride!"

Maybe it was the anxiety of the moment, or perhaps someone else had entered the room. Maybe it was Arthur! He could have sensed her distress. After all, it had been a huge strain on her, sitting by the deathbed for so many hours. Arthur had warned her to call for him if his mother showed even the slightest change.

Yes! There was change all right.

Who *was* this man who was calling out to her in such a loud, demanding, and disrespectful manner? She strained her thoughts. It was a familiar voice, but Margaret, exhausted from her nursing duties, did not immediately recognize it.

"Step aside," the gentleman ordered.

Margaret bolted toward the door, missed it, and instead hit the bedroom wall face-forward as she took a spin back around to study the mysterious figure.

He was dressed in his signature gray suit as she fought the reality of the scene. It was Willie, the husband of Nelly and the father-in-law that she had so feared! His intimidating personality had frightened her at the engagement party he and Nelly had hosted for Arthur and her. Margaret had made excuses not to be near him when he was alive. He made her feel uncomfortable and insufficient as a wife for his treasured son.

Willie had been dead for five years and had passed with a great sadness at having to leave his fair and vivacious Nelly. It had been five years to the day since the family had laid him to rest in Savannah's prestigious Laurel Grove Cemetery on a crisp fall afternoon. It had been five years since she had held the arm of

Nelly as the widow reached over the side of the casket and placed a rose on her deceased husband.

Yes! Willie was dead, but his image was very much alive in that moment and standing just a few feet in front of her. Could it be that his years spent in heaven (or hell) had made him whole again?

Too frightened to scream, Margaret watched as he moved closer to the stiff body of his beloved.

"Nelly," he proclaimed. "Come. Come with me so we shall be together forever."

And with his command, Nelly opened her eyes and was lifted up from the bed and into the arms of her husband before vanishing as a couple for one final time. Margaret gasped, as if she were trying to call them back.

"Wait! I, uh, who . . . where . . . don't . . . ," she stammered.

And then she glanced toward the bed. The ashen, thin body was still and blue.

Margaret mustered a scream so loud that blood rushed to her head and caused her to faint and fall back against the clock she so loved. Arthur dashed up the stairs and into the room. Cradling her head in his lap and grasping her hands, he called for the doctor.

It was a brand-new hat, fresh from a factory in New Jersey. Willie had purchased it to wear on the eve of his graduation from Yale. Black and stiff and tall, the top hat was a symbol of success in its day.

For a Southern boy born into a prominent and wealthy family, completing studies at an Ivy League college warranted a first-class dress-up celebration. He was going to put on his best in hopes of meeting the right young woman.

Nelly had dreamt of finding a man like Willie, strong and debonair. Every detail of that day was premeditated, even down to her swift arrival into his strong arms.

Sliding down the staircase following the Yale graduation ceremony seemed like a good thing to do at the time. She could get to the bottom floor quickly, while at the same time clean the railing with her new dress. Her mother would probably scold her for a lack of manners; nonetheless, and as always, she pursued her whim. She almost always pursued her whim. That's what made Nelly special. She was not a woman of her time, but one who might well could have debuted in the next century as a liberated female.

So, down she went, speedily catching the dust from the railings in her crinoline and landing right into the outstretched arms of Willie. The force of her body knocked his hat off and her feet hit the floor, braking like a wild horse. The socialites of Savannah would have never approved of such behavior.

"Why, Madam, whatever possessed you to do such a thing?" Willie asked. "Now look what you've done to my new hat!" And with that, he clasped her hand and whisked her out onto the dance floor, whirling and laughing.

Willie (the namesake of William Washington Gordon I) soon wed the comedic Eleanor "Nelly" Kinzie in a grand ceremony in their hometown of Savannah. The Yale grad first supported his new wife as an astute and personable cotton factor and merchant. Later he became a partner in a prominent firm prior to establishing his own company, which he later named Gordon & Gordon.

Politics and war often separated Willie from the love of his life. As a member of the Georgia Hussars, a Savannah cavalry troop, he became a lieutenant in the Civil War. Following the war he served with the Georgia State Cavalry, and he served in the Georgia House of Representatives from 1884 to 1890. He entered the War of 1898 as brigadier general of the United States Volunteers. After that war, he remained politically devoted to the Democratic Party.

After Nelly and Willie married, the couple moved into the Wayne-Gordon House, where they also lived with the elder Mrs. Gordon, Sarah, until she passed away there. By 1861 the couple had two children: Eleanor, born in 1858, and Juliette (nicknamed Daisy), born in 1860, who later founded the Girl Scouts of America. Nelly and Willie later had four more children.

The couple's love was strong, and Nelly was steadfast in her devotion to her husband, who was taken away from her by war. During the Civil War years, Willie was lauded as one of the South's finest soldiers. His unit was part of the Jefferson Davis legion during the Virginia campaign, and Nelly spent many nights lying awake and wondering about the fate of her beloved. As the war progressed, her longing for news of his whereabouts led to a plan that would lead her to him. Nelly turned her charm on generals Robert E. Lee and William Tecumseh Sherman to help her locate Willie. When she discovered that he had been in Virginia and later made his way south to Charleston, she convinced Sherman to allow her to travel to Charleston armed with a truce flag to bid Willie farewell. She and her children headed north again. (Some say it was her flirtations that inspired Sherman to spare Savannah.)

It was that same high-spirited Nelly, too, who was still fond of sliding down staircases. She eventually returned to Savannah to the home she loved. For many years she slid down the stairs of her beautiful mansion, the home where she and Willie raised their family.

Willie's death left a passionate void in Nelly's heart. She grieved until her soul ached with such a deep pain that would never cease. Five years later, in the heat of summer, Nelly became ill as she planned the birthday party of her eldest child. At first she felt as though she couldn't stomach food of any kind. Then, suddenly, a sickness overcame all that remained of her. Her loss of appetite was accompanied by a severe headache, and then nausea consumed her aching body, her skin became jaundiced, and she developed a raging fever. The town's physician declared her terminally ill. It was a dreadful death, and her family could not stand to see her suffer. They stayed with her as long as they could, watching her die a slow and tormenting path to eternity.

Margaret rubbed her eyes, thinking they might be heavy with sleep and that she was possibly hallucinating. When she came to, she pushed Arthur's hands and the smelling salts away and began questioning her own sanity. Then, reality set in.

She had just spoken to a dead man who was standing in the room of her husband's dead mother. Willie had been a gentleman of the highest sorts, but was far too stiff to warm up to and, at times, his wit could be unpleasant. Today, Margaret had trembled as she watched his arms extend and then caress his beloved, entreating her to join him in eternity. Standing poised and dapper, he had proclaimed his mission a second time, louder and more authoritatively.

"What's all the commotion, dear? Is it Mother?" Arthur whispered, thinking his voice might calm her. Margaret, who by this time was sprawled on the floor, sobbed with fear and desperation in what appeared to be a semiconscious state.

"Your father . . . your father. He was just here."

"My dear, you are surely experiencing the mental toll from being in this room far too long."

"Arthur, I wish I could believe your mother is with him now. Arthur, you don't understand. I've seen your father, and he is alive and well."

"Nonsense! We must leave before the others find you in this upset condition. They've been through enough already."

"I'm sorry, Arthur."

Margaret flung her arms around him, seeking comfort in her fear. Then together they slowly walked into the hallway and down the great winding staircase to tell the others, who had gathered in their mother's favorite room, the parlor.

At the foot of the stairs stood Cicero, wide-eyed with fear and disbelief. Cicero was the family's loyal butler and friend, and he, too, began describing the surreal reunion he had just experienced when he saw his former boss descend the stairs. His head was humbly bent and he raised his eyes, which were pouring tears, to the couple. Reaching out with trembling hands, he muttered, "Shake this hand, Mr. Arthur. The General, he just clasped this old hand of mine. He came down these stairs here with his bride, just as plain as you and Miss Margaret."

Arthur's face was stricken with a stark paleness.

"What?" he exclaimed loudly to Cicero, who was partially deaf.

"The General said to me, 'Well, Cicero, I have been able to come get Miss Nelly. I am here a while longer.' Then, let's see, he said something instead of good-bye, '*Au revoir.*'"

Then Cicero said that Willie gave him a salute, and he and Miss Nelly went out the door as if a buggy were waiting to whisk them away to a social gathering.

Arthur turned to Margaret, finally believing the story she and Cicero had told.

Cicero patted Margaret on the back and concluded, "The General was always so proud of you, missus. He looked well and happy now, Mr. Arthur . . . happier than I have ever seen him. I'm not going to say anything about this to anybody, but I reckon you'd like to know. The General came to fetch his missus himself."

Chuckling at the sight of their dear loved ones attempting to make sense of it all, Willie and Nelly, arm-in-arm, had vanished to the realm of heaven awaiting them.

Oftentimes, a gentle strumming of the zither will prompt Nelly's appearance, and she will waltz with joy through the main parlor and turn, smiling, toward her unsuspecting guests. Occasionally Nelly and Willie will return to the house together, and employees will catch a quick glimpse of Nelly sliding down the banister, which has been restored to its original charm. In this house—where the founder of the Girl Scouts, Juliette Gordon Low, once lived—joy and laughter fill the rooms at the day's end. It is said that the deceased family takes over the home when all the employees have left and that they carry on as if they were alive. By sunrise, they all climb the stairs back to heaven's glory.

As you tour the home, don't be surprised if you feel the General's chilled hand touching your own. According to Cicero, his grip remains strong to this day.

This story was paraphrased from its original form and used with permission by the Juliette Gordon Low Birthplace, Savannah, Georgia.

THE WAVING GIRL

On the east end of rustic River Street stands a striking visual tribute to one woman and her devotion to all who enter Savannah's port by water. Created by the famous artist Felix D. Weldon, who created the Iwo Jima Monument, it stands nine feet tall in the form of a beautiful raised sculpture of a wavy-haired young lady. In her elongated hands, she clutches a flag-like piece of fabric that appears to be fluttering in the breeze. Beside her stands a trusty dog looking out onto the harbor. A small lantern lies at her feet. For forty-four years, this lady never missed a ship, waving her handkerchief by day and the gas lantern each evening as ships sailed by after the sun set. Florence Martus, whose beloved maritime ritual defined Southern hospitality, may be Savannah's only unofficial greeter to captains and crews as they arrived in vessels of all sizes. But there's a story that has never been written and signs that a younger and forelorn Florence is still on duty, forty-six feet above the treacherous entrance to the river in the country's smallest lighthouse. Look for her when the moon is full and its light illuminates a pathway on the water that leads to the little lighthouse on Cockspur Island.

There's an art to navigating the muddy Savannah River.

For captains of the massive cargo ships venturing into the Port of Savannah, that art lies in the steady hands and wisdom of Savannah's professional pilots, who know these waters like the brand of coffee they sip to keep them awake on long nights at sea.

Although there is plenty of depth, the entrance into the South Channel of the Savannah River is narrow, with obstacles that are often unseen by even the wisest captain. Even when equipped with sophisticated navigation devices, it can be a treacherous ride for the inexperienced. Many of those careless captains occasionally get swallowed up by sharp and powerful demons called jetties that appear on the north and south side of the entrance. "Make sure you're careful among those jetties," a crusty old shrimp boat captain remarked. "The markers are confusing, especially at night. If you're coming from the big island over the short stretch of sea, you can't see them. If it's dark, you'll run over them. These hazards are meant to guide. But they have been known for years to tear up a boat, injure its passengers, and bring stark reality into the minds of overzealous sailors who think they know it all."

As the Atlantic Ocean waves merge into the channel at the mouth of the river, a strong current churns unmercifully, spewing foamy caps like beaters turning plain egg whites into thickened meringue peaks. In short, there is enough power generated in that little stretch of waterway to steer a blind boater into the dangerous stretch of water. If one survives a bout with these floating landmines called jetties, odds are, the vessel won't be afloat for long, for the current will suck a stricken boat into a small chasm and beneath the waves into a black sea to lie upon the muddy bottom for eternity.

That's what happened to Andrew Kellum, a bright young Yankee naval officer who had sampled the shores of Savannah and met a beautiful young lady named Florence walking her collie, one summer night.

Sea breezes whip around the corner of Cockspur Island in sync with lapping waves that slap the oyster-laden shoreline. The picturesque small plot of land is often covered by water as it lies low in the south channel of the Savannah River on Lazaretto Creek. It's a magical place where gulls sweep the skyline and kite-boarders zig-zag through the creek throughout the day. At dusk, open-air boats joggle the dolphins as tourists snap photos of their circuslike antics. As shrimp boats and other vessels maneuver the channel that leads from the Savannah River into the picturesque creek, that tiny slither of land once stood proudly, a guiding light for ships as they entered the channel heading to the port.

The Cockspur Island Lighthouse stands on the tip of an islet and, at one time, was a captain's most reliable form of navigation. The iconic structure is forty-six feet tall, made of bricks marking the channel. And although it's no longer used, there are ghosts that whisper about days gone by in a place that once evoked terror and heartbreak.

On Cockspur Island, which is little more than a sandbar, this lighthouse has served its followers well. And with all its beauty, it has taken a lashing by hurricanes and barely survived the bombardments of Union troops in the American Civil War. The first brick tower was built between March 1837 and November 1839 and served as a temporary day-marker for sailors. Declared insufficient for the growing needs of Savannah's busy port, in 1848, a well-known New York architect was asked to design and oversee the building of a full-fledged station that would become an even stronger beacon. John Norris, the acclaimed architect who designed many of Savannah's grand homes and buildings, saw to it that a proper lighthouse keeper's house was built just steps away from the lighthouse. It was a simple cottage with a main living and dining area and two small bedrooms. The lighthouse was painted white, and hence, Norris installed a fixed white light that operated off five meager lamps with fourteen-inch reflectors to shine out into the channel. His light would be visible for nine miles and would not be extinguished until two hurricanes and war saw to its demise.

On August 7, 1869, Florence Margaret Martus was born in the cottage where her father lived as he tended to the lighthouse. Her mother, the former Cecelia Decker of Philadelphia, was the perfect wife to this lighthouse keeper, a man whose job rarely allowed him off-duty time. Evenings were quiet in the Martus household as the sounds of the pounding seas and, less often, gentle waves proved the only sign of nearby life. The family had few friends as a visit to the Martus camp was dependent on the winds and tides. If the tide was too low, visits by boat weren't possible. If the tide was too high, it covered the strip of rock and sand, cutting the small structure off from the world, except by boat.

A German immigrant, Charles Martus could hardly believe that his luck had turned positive. Burdened with anxiety at being in a new country and facing grim chances of finding employment, his pleasant demeanor and crafty skills as a handyman had landed him the job as lighthouse keeper in a setting that he saw as idyllic.

For Florence and her brother, George, growing up on tiny Cockspur Island was both joyful and frightening. On beautiful spring afternoons when the gentle breezes cooled their natural playground, they entertained themselves with games of hide-and-seek, fishing, or crabbing. But when the storm winds blew off the Atlantic and enveloped the island with angry skies and screeching howls, it could be frightening and lonely. They were only a year apart with George being the oldest, and many would say they were more like best friends than brother and sister.

At the age of twelve, family life in the lighthouse was threatened when an enormous storm pushed the water ashore and rose twenty-three feet above sea level. The surge was enough to ruin their special home and send the family to a makeshift shelter — a small, two-story cottage within Fort Pulaski that would remain as a lightkeepers home until the 1900s and the next life-changing event would occur.

As they grew into their teens, the pair created activities relying on nature to supply their entertainment. The bottoms of Florence's feet were rough from traipsing barefoot around the house at low tide. As a small girl, she had played with her dolls on the sandy sidewalk her father had leveled. It was a clean path that progressed straight down to the lighthouse, free of the sharp spurs for which the island was named. Now they had land in a shelter that was tall enough to stay dry.

Florence and her brother collected shells at low tide and occasionally swam, staying close to the shore, when the water was gentle. There were days when he assisted his father, stirring grout to its proper thickness and replacing brick that had loosened from age. Those were the days Florence loved best. She loved climbing the staircase to the top of the lighthouse, where she would sit for hours dangling her legs below the rails and watching cargo-laden ships making their way into the Port of Savannah. She was queen of the island, and the waving captains who passed her by were her most adoring fans.

With tanned arms and legs and light-brown hair that was becoming more and more bleached by the sun, Florence evolved into a shapely young lady, as her adoration for the salty breezes and passing vessels grew. All was well until the day her father suddenly passed away from a ravaging fever that overcame all efforts to cure him. As the family grieved and planned his funeral in the small cottage on Cockspur Island, a young man named Andrew Kellum knocked on the door of the lighthouse keeper's cottage.

"Um, hello," said the spry and youthful Kellum, whose skin was leather-like and blistered by the sun. "My fishing boat has run aground, and I could sure use a drink of water."

Florence quickly fetched her mother and brother, and the three of them began pampering the red-faced Kellum, ecstatic that a visitor had ventured to their little island home in the midst of their pain.

"Enjoy your stay here as well as our hospitality," Florence said. "You must wait until the change of the tide, and then you will find that your vessel will float right out of here."

Florence had seen it happen many times from the top of her favorite perch. Her expertise was like that of the most well-trained helmsman, and Kellum was amused by her knowledge of the sea.

"I have taken a job for one of the wealthy cotton merchants in town to bring fish to the market in the square. This is not my boat," Kellum said. "As you can see, I haven't caught any fish so this will possibly be my final day here on the job. I will stay until the tide changes, but I must see you again."

And with that, he dozed off on the small love seat leaving stains of his sweat on the fabric. A few hours later, he awakened to the sounds of the gulls fetching their morning catch on the glimmering Lazaretto Creek. As far as he could tell, the family was asleep in their bedrooms so he quietly and hastily crept out into the salty air and piercing sunlight. As he made his way down the sandy sidewalk and into the surf toward his vessel, he glanced up toward the top of the lighthouse. There, he saw the outline of beautiful Florence, facing toward the river, waving her apron frantically at a passing ship. She turned and looked down at him while giggling, "Bon voyage, you silly Andrew!"

Kellum could tell the tide was high enough to prompt his swift departure.

"You are so pretty," he shouted. "May I take you out tomorrow eve?"

With head thrown back, her laughter drowned the maddening squawks of the birds fighting for their breakfast. Florence replied, "Yes! Be gone now and return that boat before they toss you in prison for stealing." As he sailed away, she loosened the tie on her apron and waved it to him until he faded into the horizon, now illuminated by the glowing sun.

It was 1887 and Tybee Island was now on the map for tourists seeking the sun and sand near their Southern homeplaces. The Central of Georgia Railroad had successfully connected Tybee with Savannah, becoming key to endless holidays. Savannah's wealthiest had built nearly 400 homes and Florence was a blossoming young women. Kellum and Florence enjoyed spending long days lying on the beach and dancing the evening away in open-air venues hailed as high-class Tybee resorts.

Evenings were magical and filled with laughter and long kisses. There were big bands playing there on occasion, and Kellum enjoyed nothing more than leading his beloved Florence across the pier's wooden planks as the cool ocean breezes blew gently and song after song played.

Andrew was amused by Florence's passion to retreat to her lighthouse station whenever she heard a ship was sailing into Savannah's port, and he encouraged her to continue to pursue her desire for welcoming the weary ocean travelers.

In between the couple's romantic dates, Florence's mother suffered a fatal heart attack and she and her brother, George, agreed to stay and watch over the

Cockspur Lighthouse. But in between her daily duties, Florence could only think of becoming Kellum's bride and his likeness began to consume her every thought.

"What would you think about spending the rest of your life with me?" Andrew asked her timidly one evening.

Florence hesitated, and with a grim look on her face, suddenly broke into a broad smile and said, "I will live for nothing more."

Riding on the joy of hearing those words, Andrew spoke with his employer in Savannah and asked for an advance on his paycheck. Although the fishing had slowed down due to an unexpected cold spell, he had proven his loyalty and faithfulness, seeking to please his master. With barely enough change to survive, he had been taking on extra jobs at the port, unloading cargo whenever he had the chance. With all the funds he could muster, he headed into town to the silversmith, and there on an old wooden table, he scratched out a drawing of a ring he would have the jeweler make for Florence.

It was a thin silver band with hardly the width to host a sweet engraved message from him to her. Nonetheless, Andrew asked the jeweler to tap an endearing message in the tiny space. He orchestrated a moving proposal with high hopes that it would be an evening they would both never forget.

It was 1891, and George's talents were called to work at Elba Island, a small inland island closer to Savannah. Along with the Cockspur Lighthouse, his father had also assisted in the maintenance of the cottage there, and George would likely oblige. Florence would have to go with him, and she would inform Andrew of the news that evening when he arrived in his small boat to take her for a leisurely cruise down Lazaretto Creek. As she climbed the steps to the top of the place where she had grown accustomed to sitting for hours waving to hundreds of vessels going in and out of port, she paused to thank God for the many years of joy that the lighthouse had brought her.

Her family had survived a hurricane that sent them up the staircase for shelter from the rising waters and fierce winds. She had gone from a little girl to a woman very much in love in the white-bricked structure. It had been such a simple life and Florence was looking forward to sharing a new future and new home in Savannah with her beloved.

As she waited, her eyes scanned the waters for Andrew and his small boat crowned by his captivating smile. Kellum would be arriving from the north, cruising past her, loaded with fish he had caught off Tybee. The sun had set, and darkness was dangling on the edge of the sky.

The channel was unusually busy with shipping traffic both inward and outward, and long about 9 p.m., her worry turned to a sick concern.

She sat there all night, waving her lantern to every vessel that passed, hoping one would be Kellum, but in the darkness, she never saw a glimpse of the one she loved.

"We must go," George called out to her the next morning. "Our new life at Elba Island awaits!"

For the final time, Florence gazed out across the channel. She could see the sharp jetties that struck fear in the captains who were bringing their vessels into port. Trying not to think the worst, she and George packed up and made their way to their new home by a waiting tender.

Andrew had heard the news! A brother and sister by the last name of Martus were moving into the cottage at Elba Island! He was ecstatic! It would save him hours of time sailing in the inadequate fishing boat, and he couldn't wait to meet Florence there and ask her to become his wife. But the winds crossed his path from Tybee at the mouth of the river, and the churning waves in the channel had sucked him right into the jetties. He struggled with all his might to keep the boat off the dangerous rocks, but it was too late. Gashes in the side of the boat were sending the sea gushing into the vessel's belly engulfing the the last space of air. The boat was sinking. With the silver wedding ring in his pocket, he prayed aloud for his salvation until water overtook his final word. Tumbling below the surface with the boat, the water pressure pounded his eardrums, and he looked up only to visualize the face of Florence Martus before resting on the bottom of the sea beneath the heavy boat.

Florence's beautiful blonde hair turned brassy red as the new home was much more shaded than Cockspur Island. As she stood on the bank waving to the passing ships, never missing a single one in forty-four years, the grief of her loss festered and widened like a hurricane in warm waters. Many evenings she sat on the white-columned porch with her collie and stared blankly out to sea, dreaming of the festive and romantic evenings she spent dancing on the shores of Tybee

Island. Each day she wrote of her pain in a diary that no one would ever read, as she burned the small book before her death.

Her life became an infatuation for writers from all over the country, and her home became a museum filled with trinkets and gifts from sailors and crew members. But in all those years, there was never a word from her soulmate.

She waved for the last time on June 1, 1931, from Elba Island, and she and her brother moved inland to Bona Bella on the outskirts of Savannah.

In 1909, the Cockspur Lighthouse was extinguished and today, drivers crossing over the bridge on Highway 80 East to Tybee Island will glance over to the white brick structure to observe the waves crashing against it. Most of the oyster beds beneath the lighthouse have been washed away and replaced with large rocks that protect the structure.

It is said that on a full moon evening, shadows of a shapely woman can be seen leaning over the rail waving with all her might. And on the darkest nights, a foggy light will glow from the lighthouse windows sending warmth to her lover's grave just past the entrance to Lazaretto Creek.

It was the spring of 2009 and Jeremy and his buddy, Whit, drove into Savannah from Wilmington Island with boat in tow to dive for megalodon teeth. Shark teeth hundreds of centuries old had been recovered from the waters of the Savannah River, and pushing all warnings aside, the two twenty-year-olds sought adventure.

Surprisingly, the area within the Savannah River, from the mouth toward the land opposite Elba Island, was prime fossil-diving territory. The constantly moving currents made for an ever-changing ocean floor as the sand below would shift to and fro with the waves, uncovering and recovering treasures. On a good day, one might find at least a couple of prehistoric teeth. On a more challenging day, bottle caps and beer bottles might be the only finds. But on this day, the water temperature was a stark fifty degrees and the guys donned their wet suits. Armed with navigational charts, they tossed the anchor overboard where the letter *H* designated the sand to be hard, the perfect breeding ground for their find.

The waters of the Savannah River were little more than muddy, but the divers weren't going to let that stop them. Although they couldn't see to read their tank pressure gauges or compass beneath the surface of the water, they were attentive to the swiftly changing conditions.

Taking all precautions, Jeremy dove first while Whit watched his line intently. Jeremy was a skilled solo diver and an even more experienced fossil diver.

Lowering himself deeper, Jeremy finally touched the floor. With special tools in a waterproof pouch, he stirred the sandy bottom, collecting unknown relics.

When he finally popped up, he handed Whit his find and climbed aboard.

The bag was heavy with mostly thick, wet sand that they washed off in the surf. A crab scampered off and scrambled at the floor of the boat. Whit reached down and tossed it back into the water.

And then, something amazing occurred.

To their delight, a three-inch shark's tooth fell out onto the seat of the boat. Beneath it, a weathered and bent silver, stoneless ring appeared.

"Wow! This is cool! Looks really old," Jeremy said.

"With this ring, I thee wed," Whit said jokingly. And then the two were silent.

As Jeremy studied the ring, he saw the faint outline of words on the inside of the band.

"To Flo, my waving girl forever."

"He must have run out of space," Whit said. "Maybe her name was Florence, Flo for short."

The two sat and stared at the rustic heirloom as the breeze conjured up shivers.

Suddenly, their small fishing boat jolted and they realized that the winds had forced the anchor to pull out from its grasp and the current had pushed them several feet off course.

They looked up and neither could say a word. It was in that moment, they understood they they had just discovered the mystery that instilled an overwhelming saddness in the heart of Savannah's Waving Girl, Florence Martus.

MISS JANE'S REVENGE

The beautiful home in shady Wright Square would be the perfect place for two profes-
sional brothers to take up residence. But little did they know that the former resident
kept a journal filled with terror and that they would soon find themselves talking to
the dead and defending her while a vile and deceitful husband got away with murder.

With facades that reflect modern times, the storefronts surrounding historic Wright Square appear new, with shiny glass windows that glisten in the moss-filtered sunlight. These are the places that downtown workers and residents dash into for a prescription, a cold drink, or a magazine. On the State Street side of the square stands a pharmacy, and directly behind that pharmacy once stood an eloquent home with a ghostly past.

They were an odd couple, of sorts. They were brothers, both of them handsome and single, who were trying to save a dime and, in doing so, accepted each other's unique living and sleeping habits.

Charles Jones Jr. was mayor of Savannah from 1860 to 1861. A gentleman of respectable standing, he was also a distinguished lawyer and a well-known historian. Tall and slender, Charles was an impeccable dresser with a drawl as long as the Savannah River. He had developed his accent in an age when Southern wasn't really a label. With his signature round tortoiseshell glasses and ties that were imported from London, he was easily recognizable within the realms of Savannah's social scene. A highly eligible bachelor, he was often the choice of single women, who would constantly flirt with him as he shopped in the gentlemens' tailor shops on nearby Broughton Street.

His brother, John, was studying to be a physician and relied on Charles to cook the meals and tend to the housekeeping while he worked as a resident at Candler Hospital, often staying well into the night and early morning hours. While Charles was tall and distinguished, John was a sloppy mess, perceived by some to be a misfit in spite of his distinguished profession. With his scruffy, unshaven face, John was constantly in and out of the house, spending his evenings off from the hospital with friends at the local River Street bars. Between his professional duties at the hospital and his active social life, he was rarely home, leaving Charles with a peaceful place to work and live.

In the market for the perfect house to rent, they came upon a distinguished home in an elite neighborhood called Ardsley Park, in midtown Savannah. The house had been empty for months, and other than an occasional mouse and a few spiderwebs that claimed the corners of several rooms, it would be the perfect dwelling for the brothers once they tidied it up.

Charles was an eloquent writer and enjoyed communicating with his relatives who lived up north. The home's former owner had left her furniture stored in the garret, and when Charles came upon the contents, he wrote a letter to his married sister in New Jersey describing his discoveries, stating, "With this silent room and its somber contents, the present held no companionship. The past claimed all as its own, and there was none to disturb the gloomy memories which clustered, and the gathering dust settling noiselessly there."

According to Charles, his and John's snooping had revealed some grave facts. They discovered that three sisters previously owned the house. The first sister had married and moved to the West Indies, where she later died. The second sister had died in the house of a dreadful case of malaria, leaving the third sister, Miss Jane, to live there in her own pity and loneliness. The final months of her life were so disturbing that Charles discovered it would take a complete ink refill to complete the letter.

"It is well apparent from her belongings and a diary that I am holding that long and lonely nights led her to a hasty engagement to a widower who was several years younger and had a family," he wrote. "People wondered, and the city gossips were busy with what they were pleased to term a rather strange engagement. Some smiled, others marveled, while others still safely shook their heads and predicted no good of the match."

Behind closed doors, all was not well with the newlyweds, Charles shared. With a perfect marriage shining through to the public, there were angry rants and beatings taking place almost nightly in the home that Jane was now sharing with her new husband. It seems that the bride was having second thoughts about her hasty marriage.

Clinging to the dusty diary, Charles relayed that on one particular evening, Jane was tied to a chair in the kitchen and left to starve for several days. Her husband, meanwhile, was to be found dancing with a slender blonde in Savannah's grand DeSoto Hotel's ballroom, while several of the more elite townsfolk looked on.

Suspiciously, prior to the marriage, the groom-to-be requested that Miss Jane rewrite her will to "vest her entire property in a trustee for the benefit of her intended husband's children by a former marriage." With the ceremony "scarcely over," Charles wrote, there was an "open quarrel, and it was darkly hinted by those best informed, that acts of violence were becoming more and more frequent."

Charles found copies of police reports in Miss Jane's collection and began reviewing the charges. According to the police, the couple was soon at war on a regular basis and screams, moans, and crying could be heard throughout the square, often capturing the attention of those passing by.

The Savannah police were summoned five times, and the records described scenes that started inside the house and escalated so harshly that hospital visits became more and more frequent for the thinning and abused bride. The daily newspaper began adding the couple's woes and Jane's misfortunes to their headlines: "Police Retrieve Newlywed" and "Young Wife Beaten" were among the words that lured locals to the newsstands.

One evening Charles brought the massive trunk down to the parlor so he and John could go through its contents. What they discovered were writings that revealed more dreadful events that occurred on the premises.

According to the writings, several years had passed until finally "this sorrowful and pitiful woman; wife but in name, and at best unattractive in form and feature, and without intellectual and social qualities of a high order, grew paler and more dejected until, finally, passing into a state of settled melancholy, she pined away and died a dreary, gloomy, heartbroken death."

According to the records, several townspeople turned out for a lovely funeral hosted by Jane's family in a secluded site near the water's edge in Bonaventure Cemetery, a place where mostly Savannah's elite could afford to bury its dead. Her husband was noticeably absent from the funeral gathering.

"Here we lay to rest a most remarkable woman, Miss Jane," said the Reverend Michael Bennett, of Savannah's Christ Church. "We must remember her kindness, her brave and sweet demeanor, and give our Lord thanks for bringing her into His presence where she will live forever in His kingdom of peace."

Charles and John opted to store the trunk after they had thoroughly read and suffered through the heartache of the home's former resident. And then the call came.

A grieving family member contacted Charles's law firm. The family was suspicious that their deceased loved one had been coerced into changing her will in favor of her cruel and abusive husband.

That evening Charles and John found themselves debating the task ahead over a scotch and water. For unbeknownst to her family, the brothers were holding enough evidence to convict the man of murder of his tormented wife.

"There's something odd about this thing, John," Charles said. "I'm going to put all the pieces together with our findings in this house. I am convinced that he forced her to marry him and that her modest inheritance does not belong to that man! I will defend her posthumously in order to keep his greedy hands off her things, including this house!" Soon the question of who legitimately and lawfully deserved Miss Jane's inheritance would be settled in a court of law.

Charles was a fighter, and because he had an affinity for Miss Jane, he strongly intended to win. He worked day in and day out, well into the night, to prepare for the case. Many nights he sat studying alone while his brother tended to his patients at the hospital. He couldn't forget the hell on earth that her husband put her through. He read through the newspaper clippings and turned the pages of her sad diary with the speed of a college student cramming for a final exam.

It was 2:00 a.m. As Charles worked, he paused momentarily to savor the silence. "There was no noise . . . from the outside world, and I was enjoying the golden moments," he wrote. But those golden moments were fleeting. What Charles would soon see would transform a relatively calm evening into a shocking one.

As he wrote:

About midnight I heard, or thought I heard, footsteps of someone coming from the yard into the little piazza. They then appeared to be in the piazza, and subsequently in the entry. Busied with my studies, I paid but little attention to the circumstances, presuming, in the slight notice which my thoughts for the moment took of it, that one of the servants was coming into the house for some purpose. As the sound of these footsteps reached the door just in front of me, I raised my eyes from my writing materials to ascertain who it was. Expecting to encounter a familiar face, judge of my surprise when I beheld a woman—an utter stranger to me—pausing upon the threshold—

her eyes fixed upon the floor, pale of countenance, thin, visaged, and emaciated in figure—attired in a loose morning gown of grave color, confined about the waist with a broad band of the same material, and with a large collar folding back almost to the point of either shoulder.

Her hair, sandy and lifeless in its hue, parted in the middle, was drawn tightly and plainly from the forehead and disposed behind the ears. Her countenance denoted more than sorrow. There was a wanness, a settled dejection, an absence of life and hope and love, pitiable in the extreme. Advancing, her eyes still fixed upon the floor, with slow and measured steps she passed directly in front and to the right of where I was sitting, almost touching the table.

"Are you going to help me?" she asked. "I seek revenge on this man who tarnished my soul. You and your brother will help me, I just know it. For months prior to your move here, I entered your soul, prompting you in the direction of my home."

With that, Charles jumped up from his chair in complete and utter fright and called out the name of his brother. The apparition stood there for at least three minutes, staring at him with hollow eyes and a sadness that surrounded her presence like a haze. Her anger was obvious, and yet there was a part of Charles that saw through the fear and into her broken heart.

Charles wrote, "Intensely did I watch her until she disappeared, expecting each second that she would explain the object of such an unusual visit. But never another word. I distinctly heard the tread of a slippered foot upon the modest straw laid carpet. As soon as she had entered the front parlor—which was dark—there being no light in that room—I rose from my seat and asked, 'Madame, who do you wish to see? Can I serve you in any way?' To this inquiry, there being no response, I repeated the question, and still there was no reply. Puzzled and a little provoked I took a candle from the table and went into the front parlor to ascertain who she was and what she wanted. It flashed through my mind that perchance she was some demented woman."

And then she disappeared. Charles began to search the room, looking under the sofa and even glancing upward into the chimney. Oh, where is John? he thought. I must find John.

Charles dashed out into the street and straight up the stairs to the neighbor's house. He described the woman to her and, as Charles reported, "To my surprise, she stated that the likeness presented was the exact counterpart of Miss Jane, with whom she was well acquainted, and whom she had on more than one occasion, seen in the loose morning gown, with listless air and sad countenance moving specter-like about her house, taking note of little, and seemingly holding converse only with the mournful thoughts which burdened her sorrowing and broken heart."

Charles's legal representation paid off for the family of Miss Jane. "So far as I know, or have heard, Miss Jane's perturbed spirit is now at rest," Charles wrote.

Although his words had an air of finality, Charles recalled the day when he and his brother stored Miss Jane's belongings. He raced up to the attic to retrieve the trunk that held her secrets. He frantically dug through the memories and found Miss Jane's diary. Flipping through it, he landed on the last page. On that page was written these words: "I will not rest until I have succeeded in driving my abusive husband into eternal torment. May he suffer every day of his life on earth and in the hereafter."

On the following page these words were scribbled faintly in red ink that resembled pen strikes of blood: "I am now at rest."

Many people through the years have glimpsed the frail image of a woman walking up and down State Street in the night. Following the home's demolition in 1951, she dwells peacefully in the joys of heaven and sometimes seen randomly roaming the streets of Savannah.

This story was retold from a Georgia Historical Society newsletter.

THE WRONGS OF WRIGHT SQUARE

On a typical weekday, Wright Square is one of the most serene places to enjoy Savannah's soft breezes and mild climate. Students bearing backpacks and professionals with briefcases in hand stroll with bagged lunches. In the afternoon, the sun forms defined rays that illuminate the tall monument, a tribute to William Washington Gordon, a former mayor of Savannah and the founder and president of the Central of Georgia Railroad. When the sun sets, a woman's cries and a leader's broken-hearted moans echo throughout the dimly lit place where the guilty and the innocent were hanged.

Summer vacation was finally here! Mary and John Rutland were jubilant that they would be taking their two home-schooled children, Jane and James, to Savannah, where they could study and experience Georgia history firsthand. It was a five-hour drive from their home in north Atlanta, but the monotonous trip passed quickly for the children who were absorbed in their own videos playing on their tablets.

"How much longer? When will we be in Savannah?" asked James, the younger of the two children. Like their parents, these kids were eager to discover the city their mom had taught them about in their homeschool curriculum. Savannah was Mary's hometown, and she was anxious to share it with the pair, who were now old enough to enjoy the historic port city.

Although they had booked a room on the outskirts of town to save money, the family was ecstatic about taking a self-guided walking tour through the downtown squares the very first day of their visit.

James was nine years old, and the more creative of the two children. Rambunctious and imaginative, his freckled face was accented by big green eyes. He was an avid reader for his age, and he was constantly creating scenarios involving characters he concocted—his favorite was "Cowboy Duck." As they drove and his movie played along, he paused to draw his character's endless adventures on a white notebook he carried everywhere.

About an hour from Savannah, Mary tossed James a copy of the visitors' guide sent by the Savannah Convention & Visitors Bureau. He dropped his colored pencil and began perusing the guide, which he said had "some really cool things to do." "Let's run through the squares," he said, turning the pages of the book as his dad took the exit to Savannah.

Starting their day at a quaint riverfront eatery that featured hot, homemade cheese biscuits, the Rutlands sampled Southern culinary delicacies that they had missed at home back in Atlanta. After enjoying their bowls full of hot grits with gravy and accompanying biscuits, they headed south on foot, past Johnson Square, until they found themselves staring up at the thick branches that shaded Wright Square.

"Says there's an American Indian buried over there under a big rock," James said, struggling to read words that were new to him.

As Mary, John, and Jane stood deciphering the marker on the monument that stood in the middle of the square, James disappeared, unnoticed by the family.

"Hmmmm, it says here that this square was laid out in 1733 and was named for John Percival, Earl of Egmont, who played a large part in founding the colony of Georgia. The square was renamed in 1963 after Georgia's third governor, James Wright. Oh, my! It also says there's a rock where Tomochichi, the chief of the Yamacraw, was buried! How cool is that?" Mary finished her commentary and looked around for James. She could see the top of his head behind a large rock, the site of Tomochichi's monument. He was talking to someone, and although she couldn't see who it was, her concern for his safety steered her toward the rock.

When James Edward Oglethorpe founded Savannah in 1733, he became the founder of what was known as the 13th Colony, but Oglethorpe couldn't take full credit for the discovery. Upon the shores on the bluff stood an exiled Creek man, a former leader and chief of the Yamacraw tribe, named Tomochichi.

Tomochichi and his tribe were comprised of about 200 Creek and Yamacraw Indians. The land wasn't new to them as their descendents had been there for years and many were buried there. When Tomochichi met Oglethorpe, they became close friends, and it is said that he even accompanied Oglethorpe to England to meet King George.

Tomochichi was truly instrumental in the founding of Savannah, helping keep peace within the new city and its new citizens. He was near ninety years old when he became ill and died of unknown causes. His body was brought to Wright Square where he was buried, rightfully placed, in the center of the square.

But his body wouldn't rest there.

Marked by a pyramid-like stack of stones, in the year of 1883, The Central of Georgia Railroad Company disturbed the gravesite in lieu of a more formal monument to its founder, William Gordon, who had recently died. But what happened to the remains of Tomochichi? No one knows.

Nellie Gordon, the daughter of the railroad founder, wouldn't have such. Understanding the role that the Yamacraw leader played in the founding of Savannah, she and the members of the Colonial Dames of America thought it was only proper to redeem the tribute to his service. So, for a single dollar, the Stone Mountain Company shipped a large piece of granite ... a boulder of sorts ... to Savannah, and it was placed and encircled with arrowheads near the center monument, where it remains.

To Alice Riley the square's name was unimportant. Wright Square was the place where she, a mother to a newborn son, would die in a brutal and public manner. It was the square where she would become the first woman in Georgia to die by hanging.

Around 1733, Alice, an Irish convict and indentured servant, and her friend Richard White united in a case of greed that would lead to their horrific public demise in a square that was reserved for hangings. These two self-indulgent partners in crime had traded their freedom for free passage to the New World. When they landed in Savannah, they met Will Wise, a penniless man who had been granted permission to sail from England to Savannah to become part of the new mission started by General James Oglethorpe. Wise, a British criminal, was going to be given a second chance in this new place.

When Wise embarked on a sailing vessel in 1733, he was broke, but armed with mischief that would rock the boat and all who were aboard. Little did he know, however, that shortly after he landed in Savannah, he would render his soul into the evil hands of Alice Riley and Richard White.

Wise was bringing trouble of his own. During the three-month voyage, it was discovered that he had misrepresented a "woman of the town," calling her his daughter, and successfully smuggled her onto the ship. According to a Savannah newspaper, his actions "generated great commotion aboard ship."

With Wise already compromising his reputation, the trustees ordered him sent back to England, afraid that he might become a troublemaker in the new colony. However, despite the trustees' orders, General Oglethorpe allowed him to remain in Georgia, and on December 16, 1733, Wise started his new life on Hutchinson Island, just across the river from Savannah, where he would launch new passions—possibly farming—and begin working toward a life of prosperity.

The island, named for Archibald Hutchinson, a friend of General Oglethorpe's, was nearly seven miles long and a mile wide at the widest point, and provided Wise with the privacy he sought.

Wise set up housekeeping in a small wood-frame structure that was abandoned when he arrived. As he worked to repair it and make it his own, he suffered a fall from the roof and became permanently disabled. Shortly thereafter the trustees allotted him two indentured servants, Alice Riley and Richard White.

Reports of Wise's demeanor vary, but several agree that his handicap made him an evil man who often abused his servants. Alice and Richard became the butt of his anger, and they spent many nights locked up in an outhouse that Wise had built for slaves. As the days passed, they hated him more and more.

Morning baths brought Wise his greatest pleasure—with the exception of his last one. On the morning of March 1, 1734, according to state records, Wise called White to assist him in dressing and combing his hair to enable him to place his wig on smoothly. As was his usual practice, he leaned over the side of his bed. Alice brought in a bucket of water. White entered the room to assist and quickly twisted Wise's neckerchief to strangle him.

Alice and Richard took great pleasure as the crime unfolded and laughed throughout the horrible scene.

"He's finally getting what he deserves," Alice said. "How do you like your bath today, mister?" she asked jokingly. Her dialogue continued as she neatly and efficiently seized the choking and coughing man's head and plunged it into the bucket of water, putting an end to Wise's reign over the servants, who by this time were celebrating their freedom.

The next day, citizens flocked to get reports from the daily record. A recount from a 1734 newspaper article described the scene: "& he being ver weak it Soon Dispatched him." Pleased that he no longer had to worry about Wise and his antics, General Oglethorpe nonetheless had Alice arrested on the spot. White escaped on foot to the Isle of Hope, but he was soon caught and returned to Savannah's wretched jail.

Although they maintained their innocence, Alice and Richard appeared before the state bailiffs' court and were sentenced to death by hanging. Behind the scenes, townspeople were gossiping about the fate of the lovers. While in prison, it was determined that Alice was pregnant with Richard's child.

Publicly pleading for her life, Alice asked to be spared on behalf of her unborn child. She was granted a delay until she gave birth, to a son. And while Alice died at the gallows on January 19, 1735, in Wright Square, some say she hung for all to see for three solid days. Following the removal of her body, Richard shared the same scaffold as Alice. He died quickly as his neck snapped beneath a black hood, and his body flailed until it became stiff. Ironically their son, James, lived only a few weeks beyond the executions.

"James! James! Get right back over here!" shouted Mary, this time focusing not on Savannah's history, but on how she would discipline her disobedient child, who was ignoring her commands.

James glanced around the corner of the odd-shaped rock and motioned to his mother with his index finger pointed up, as if to say, "Just give me a minute."

"My name is James. That's my mama back there," he said to the woman who was near tears. "My mama said not to talk to strangers. I don't like you. You're scaring me, I'm gonna call my mama."

"I've been looking for you," the woman said. "My name is Alice, and this is where I died. Now, James, you have been returned to me. My, what a handsome lad you are. You favor your father, but I see myself in your eyes. Come! We shall be together from this day forward."

James thought for a moment and then turned around to face his mom, who was by now walking the quick steps of a short-tempered mother.

"James, what have you been doing, and why did you ignore me?" Mary asked.

"I was talking to a dead woman named Alice who thought I was her son. She said the scariest thing. She told me to look up in the branches here in the square, and when I find a bare spot—a place where no moss is hanging—I'll be looking at the very place where her dead body dangled before the townsfolk. She has plucked every thread of moss from that very spot."

Mary grabbed James's hand and walked briskly toward a trolley they were departing on that was about to close its doors. "Hurry up, mama," said Jane. "We've got your seats. Hurry! We're about to leave!" After barely catching the trolley that was, by now, hailing its stray boarders, Mary's mind began to wander. She must discuss this behavior with James's pediatrician when they returned home.

As they climbed aboard, Mary glanced back into Wright Square. The trees were rustling in a gentle wind that seemed to be embracing the beautiful square.

As Mary sat down on the wooden bench with her son, the trolley started to move. And then she turned to see something very strange. Hardly able to comprehend what her eyes saw, she fixated on a giant live oak that stood on the southeast side of the square. On the tree she noticed a thick branch that was hanging without so much as a single strand of moss. The other branches of that very tree were heavily laden with the Spanish moss that was so prevalent in Savannah. Her thoughts reverted to James's conversation, that by now had moved on to stories of pirates fighting his make-believe character, Cowboy Duck. Perhaps he was on to something.

Maybe that really was the place where Alice's and Richard's blood was spilled as they hung lifeless from the tree. Maybe this was the place where moss would never hang.

"James, can you tell me what the woman you were talking to on the other side of the grave looked like?" she asked.

"She was real pale, like my paper," he said, holding his drawing pad up to her. "She had on a black dress like a witch."

The trolley leaned as it rounded another corner and then James turned to her again, this time, tugging on her sleeve.

"Oh, and there were these sores that went around her whole neck. Her head hung to one side."

Later that evening, the family revisited Wright Square, the home of a terrible hanging and the very place where the body of a special city founder named Tomochichi, may, or may not, still lie beneath the monument in tribute to the late Central of Georgia Railroad's founder. And while there is a large granite boulder off to the side in his honor, it is not known where the body of Chief Tomochichi rests to this day.

And to this day, an heir of sadness hangs over Wright Square like the moss that encompasses it, bleeding the stories that have haunted Savannah's visitors for centuries.

BONAVENTURE: NO WAY OUT

There is an overwhelming aura of peacefulness that engulfs the senses as one passes through the gates of Bonaventure Cemetery in Savannah. Spread out like the noble grounds of the lush Southern plantation that it once was, the beautiful cemetery lies along the shores of the Wilmington River and provides a resting place for many prominent Savannahians. A mere three miles from the city's historic downtown, Bonaventure is both lovely and daunting. Although angels, cherubs, and all the other symbols of good reside there, when the moon is full and its light is shining on the waters like a pathway to heaven, the cemetery turns eerie, and there are days when one wrong turn inside can transform a mundane visit into a chilling (and surprising) discovery.

Grant was glad that the burial services for his friend, Don Stevens, had been scheduled for the afternoon. He would plan to leave his office around one o'clock, swing by his favorite eatery for a quick lunch, and head straight home after the service. It had been a crazy morning, and it seemed that nothing was going his way.

A dashing, handsome, and much-sought-after single attorney, he had no obligations that evening, except for a quick review of a civil suit that was going to court the next morning.

Dressed in what he termed "funeral attire," Grant had inadvertently forgotten his tie, and in Savannah, attending the final rite for a friend required a strict dress code. "Just another thing to go awry," he thought. His black leather jacket would have to cover the fashion faux pas, as it was too late to retrieve a tie. Standing in front of the antique mirror that he had installed in his office restroom, he splashed some cologne behind his ears, took one last look, and decided that his efforts to ready himself for the upcoming funeral would have to do, regardless of the rules of the social dress police.

His law offices were slammed with cases trying to settle before the holidays. And though it was certainly no picnic, Grant was looking forward to breathing the fresh air and partaking of the stunning scenery at Bonaventure Cemetery, while also paying respects to his friend, who had died of a rare form of bone cancer.

After grabbing his keys, he caught the elevator down to street level and crossed over to his battered but beloved BMW that was parked around the square. He drove to the eatery just minutes away, thinking of what he was going to order.

As he spun into a place right in front of the downtown tavern, he reached into his pocket for his cell phone and discovered that it was missing.

"Man," he thought. "I shouldn't have left in such a rush."

By now his list of "things forgotten" was growing, but Grant was hungry enough to overlook it all. Stepping into B. Matthews, a favorite Savannah pub, he waved to a colleague who was seated alone by the window and checked out the day's specials.

Grant enjoyed his quiet lunches at B. Matthews, which claimed to be the oldest tavern in Savannah. The rustic decor, working fireplace, and friendly waitstaff offered old-time ambiance along with his favorite Savannah lunch, a black-eyed pea cake sandwich. He would enjoy himself while reflecting on the well-lived life of his deceased friend. Little did he realize that as he slowly devoured his sandwich, the lengthy procession was already making its way from the funeral home on Savannah's south side toward the gates of Bonaventure Cemetery.

Without a cell phone, Grant had no way of checking the time. The battery in his 1999 BMW B3 had recently died. After he recharged it, nothing worked. The clock was set to zero. And worst of all, according to the owner's manual, a special "radio code" was required to get the clock and radio operating again. This security feature was built into BMWs to keep people from stealing the radios. Unfortunately, this was an old car and that code was long lost. After gobbling the last bite of his sandwich, he asked for the bill and hastily paid it, jumped in his car, and headed east. As he rode in silence to the services, he prepared himself mentally for his final good-bye to his friend.

Bonaventure Cemetery has been known to distract many a funeralgoer, and Grant was no exception. Turning slowly into the gated entryway, he was instantly mesmerized by the subtle shades of gray on that cold and windy day. Stopping to study the scene, he wished he owned a more sophisticated camera, or at least had his cell phone camera.His mind reverted to like images, with like tones of gray that were reminiscent of a Jack Leigh photograph. (Leigh had made a fortune with his "Bird Lady" photo that graced the cover of the best-selling book *Midnight in the Garden of Good and Evil*.)

Stopping to survey the cemetery before him was a brilliant gesture. The thick live oaks and hanging Spanish moss were a perfect contrast to the graying tombstones and monuments, and a black-and-white photographer would have had another prize-winning shot on that gloomy afternoon. It seemed that the charcoal setting was enveloping his car. He chuckled, pretending that he was cruising through an episode of *The Twilight Zone.* "Someone should make a movie here," he said to himself, then chuckled, "Someone already has."

As he followed the narrow, winding road, his pauses became more frequent. The treasures of Bonaventure were unfolding before him in a myriad of epitaphs inscribed with poetry and scriptures, and Grant was reading them all as he cruised slowly by each family plot.

Section C, Lot 24: JOHN STODDARD, EMIGRATED JULY 25TH, 1870, AGED 70. 'FOR HE LOOKED FOR A CITY WHICH HATH FOUNDATIONS, WHOSE BUILDER AND MAKER IS GOD.'

"Wow," he mumbled quietly, as if he were standing behind the tee at a PGA golf tournament, afraid to speak for fear of admonishment.

Farther down the road, he stopped to read the fading script on the marker for William Eugene: WERE NOT FOR THE SWEETEST BUD THAT IS MISSING FOR IT FELL ASLEEP ONLY TO WAKE MORE BRIGHT AND BEAUTIFUL IN THE ARMS OF JESUS.

Soon, he forgot all about the time.

Owned by the City of Savannah since 1907, Bonaventure has been the subject of writers and historians. "Because of Bonaventure's beauty, death is robbed of half its horror," said one writer. Echoing praise of the beautiful grounds, another wrote, "Here, man can calmly sleep the sleep of death, fanned by the swaying breezes, gentle breath, the dreamless sleep—the sleep eternal laid Darkly [*sic*] shrouded beneath thy cooling shade."

Ask those who oversee the grounds to contradict these images of peace, and they'll vehemently deny and put to rest any negativity associated with this distinguished setting for the dead. "There are no ghosts at Bonaventure," they'll say.

Once the bustling plantation homes of the Tattnall and Mullryne families, the name Bonaventure (which means "good fortune") was bestowed on the flourishing land, and perhaps that name is just one of the many elements that have contributed to the cemetery being known as a scenic place of peace and joy.

Savannahians sometimes joke that some people are actually "dying to get to Bonaventure." Take the story of the clergyman who killed himself within the gates in hopes of being buried there. It appeared in a *New Orleans Picayune* article by a woman named Belle. According to Belle, the clergyman "was smitten with the beauty of death" and plunged into the Wilmington River.

When all is said and done, the marks of evil are often lured by the darkness, revealing mysteries after the gates are closed.

As Grant continued his journey into the illustrious riverside cavern for the dead, memories of his friend were becoming fainter as the light of day began to fade.

His feet hit the brakes at the next bend in the road. The sign said SECTION H. Grant decided to stop and explore.

The sun was starting to set, and its rays were piercing through the gaps between the dangling moss and thick oak branches, illuminating the monuments in waves of light. To his right, Grant could see diamonds dancing on the glimmering river. To his left, there was a silence that was undisturbed by man or beast. The setting was indeed idyllic.

Standing beside his car, Grant scanned the grounds for any sign of life, or perhaps a burial in progress. That was the reason he was there. But like so many who visit this graveyard, he succumbed to the beauty of the moment that often swallows the intentions of funeralgoers, most of whom never reach the intended service in time.

Straight ahead, he spotted the image of a beautiful woman resting on the steps of a marble sculpture. Rising out of the stone stairway was a cross. It was getting cold, and Grant zipped up his leather jacket, forgetting all about the tie he had left at home.

"Hello," he said.

The woman turned to him without saying a word, straightening the creases of her flowing dress.

"I'm trying to find the Stevens' funeral."

In an instant and in defiance of Grant's inquiry, the woman looked away, continuing to ignore him. She sat staring out into the grounds that were by now turning to dark.

As Grant slowly proceeded toward the monument and the woman sitting at its foot, he was taken aback by the sound of pianos and violins. It was music, and it was coming from the speakers inside his BMW. The radio had been silenced when the battery died, and those speakers hadn't worked in years.

"I've been waiting for you," the woman finally said. "Come dance with me."

As she stood, the woman held out her arms. In the background, Grant heard the music, as if there were a party going on.

So taken with her, he spun around and began his trek toward the river and her embrace.

"I wore this for you," she said.

Grant's gait turned into a slow jog toward the woman on the marble staircase. Just as he reached out to receive her, she turned, walked back toward the monument, sat down, and turned to stone.

Filled with a jarring sense of shock intermingled with sheer panic, Grant bolted to the BMW, cranked up the engine, and with trembling hands turned on the headlights. An arrow pointing toward Section H prompted him to speed in the other direction. He had to escape. Revving up the car and looking back and forth for an exit sign, he found himself getting deeper and deeper into the cemetery. Around and around, he drove, trying not to disturb the peace of the resting dead, yet afraid that he would be trapped inside for the night.

Frantically spinning his wheels, Grant veered left, then right. Looking ahead, he spotted an arrow. It read SECTION H. By now it was dark. And all roads led back to the place where he had first seen the woman.

If only he had his cell phone, he could call for help.

But there was no cell phone. And there was no help.

Trying to compose himself, he noticed some lights in the distance. For the sake of his sanity, Grant made one last attempt to escape by car before parking and taking off on foot.

As he watched intently, he noticed a truck ahead, moving slowly, spilling dirt from its tailgate. To his right, he read a wooden sign with the name STEVENS written in script. As he neared the vehicle ahead, he saw a similar sign lying in the rear of the truck. It fell off the tailgate, and as the truck slowed, one of the men inside jumped out to retrieve the sign.

Relieved to see that he wasn't alone, he leaned back in his seat. So much for making the funeral. After all, nothing this day had gone his way.

Grant followed the truck which led him to the exit gate, where the driver waved him on and out to Bonaventure Road and civilization.

Who was the woman sitting on those marble steps? And where did the music come from? Grant headed back to his office, which by now was long empty. He turned on his computer and typed in the word *Bonaventure,* which he discovered meant "good fortune."

A little more searching, and there she was! The woman sitting on the marble steps was, according to Bonaventure records, Corinne E. Lawton, whose image was crafted in marble by the famed sculptor Civiletti Palormo of Italy in the year 1879, a year when "wines, cordials, bitters, syrups, and ales" ads from Stults & Company importers were advertising on the front page of "The (Savannah) Times."

Bonaventure Cemetery, a place where the dead rest, had come alive that day. And not just that day, but others as well. For when the gates are closed, it has been said that there are sounds of guests enjoying a lavish party on the grounds that were once a plantation. One evening, during an extravagant dinner party at the plantation's mansion, the roof caught fire. According to the legend, the host proceeded to have the dining table and feast moved outdoors to keep the party going. The woman Grant met was, perhaps, one of those guests who had wandered off..

Grant, who was fully graced with Southern protocol, sent a handwritten note of sympathy to the Stevens family, explaining that his absence was due to an "unscheduled inconvenience." He would never admit to having been lost in the cemetery. And he would never regret spending his afternoon with the ghost of a beautiful woman whose spirit is captured in a magnificent monument near the water in Section H of Bonaventure.

GRACIE

The lifelike sculpture at the grave site of little Gracie Watson is surrounded by magnificent monuments and spacious family plots within the lush setting of Bonaventure Cemetery. Sadly, young Gracie's monument stands alone, but in a shady, serene spot that is overlooked by a glorious angel cast in stone. She is the only member of her family buried there, and her plot is seemingly orphaned. Many who visit her gravesite say they visit to comfort the soul of the child. As they come and go, they often find Gracie's cheeks adorned with tears of blood that have fallen from her marble eyes.

John Walz was ecstatic.

Standing on the icy dock in Liverpool, England, young Walz could hardly believe his luck. Facing the harsh wind in the long embarkation line, he cinched his cloth backpack with frozen hands and walked up the gangplank onto the ship that would take him to a new world and new opportunities. Walz was twenty-four, and his lanky stature, round spectacles, thick jacket, and newsboy cap gave him an intellectually youthful flair.

As an apprentice to one of the world's most highly acclaimed artists, his ticket was paid for, and that in itself was reason enough for him to take the perilous voyage. As he boarded the packet ship—a vessel that carried cargo, mail, and a limited number of passengers—apprehension replaced his excitement. But Walz didn't mind. He would gladly suffer through the rough seas and the crowded and unsanitary conditions in steerage and endure the hardships of his journey without complaint. He would see to it that the statues that were safely secured on board would be efficiently delivered to a customer waiting in Savannah.

As the ship's captain sounded a giant bell signaling their departure, the crank of the chains lifting the heavy anchor up into the ship's belly startled Walz as he tried to find a place to settle. He had brought his own bedding—a thin feather pillow and tattered blanket—realizing that there would be times when he might sleep sitting or standing up. He also realized that there would be days when his hunger would be overcome by motion sickness, discouraging him from eating. On some days the choppy waves would spill over onto the ship, making the journey uncomfortable and almost unbearable. The dark and damp cavern belowdecks wasn't exactly his idea of the way to travel, but Walz closed his eyes and began to dream of stepping onto dry land and onto the shores of a city that was bustling with promises of prosperity.

Born in Germany in 1844, John Walz was a natural artist, even in his childhood. He had the ability to create carved masterpieces from simple objects. He would pick up a piece of wood and slice away until it became something beautiful and useful, like a cane or a bench.

Walz had sampled this new country before. His parents died when he was thirteen, and he was sent to live with his only sister, who was married and residing in Philadelphia. His passion to excel eventually prompted him to return to Europe to study sculpture. Needless to say, he excelled.

As an apprentice to a renowned sculptor, Walz worked diligently on the order for large statues that was placed by Carl Brandt, the first director of the Telfair Academy (now known as the Telfair Art Museum). It was Brandt's call for artwork that opened the door for Walz to make the delivery to the beautiful city of Savannah, where more and more of Europe's wealthiest individuals were relocating.

The voyage over the Atlantic was filled with frightful moments. Strong waves tossed the vessel like a child dragging a rag doll. At times, the sea seemed to swallow the vessel. Clinging to anything he could grasp, the voyage seemed to last years and the constant motion seemed ceaseless. But when the ship finally reached the dock at Savannah's port, the sun was shining. Walz disembarked with shaky legs but a strong will. He knew his task was just beginning. He made arrangements for a horse and buggy to transport the valuable sculptures to the Telfair Academy.

Carl Ludwig Brandt was the director who had commissioned Walz's talents. His visions were to have Walz mount the stunning statues in front of the Telfair. Mounting the heavy work completed by Walz would require precision that only the artist, himself, could orchestrate. Crowds gathered to watch the mounting process, a show, of sorts. Once the process was complete, the Telfair Academy would remain an iconic Savannah wonder, even to this day.

Walz's affection for Savannah and his visions for success inspired him to open his own studio. But the studio was small, and oftentimes Walz worked all night and well into the early morning hours, so he decided to build a home on

Liberty Street where he would live and work. He was both friendly and popular, but while he was working on a project, there were days when he appeared reclusive.

Curious neighbors peered out their windows whenever Walz began a new piece of art. There was one telltale sign that signaled a new work: He would use a giant hook to lift a marble slab up to his second floor with a pulley and ropes. His neighbors respected his need for privacy; it was rare that anyone dared to call on him for friendly conversation during a project.

Walz's business flourished almost overnight as orders for monuments and architectural elements began to flow. His reputation as a sculptor of fine marble work spread throughout the city. In short, Walz became a master of his craft, and Savannahians were becoming his biggest fans.

Walz had a way of capturing the personalities of the dead. Whenever he was approached to begin work on a headstone, he spent several hours interviewing friends and relatives in order to develop a monument that would fit the needs and desires of the family. Through those interviews, he was able to successfully capture the look and personality of his subject.

Savannahians adored Walz, and the distinguished architecture of his home appealed to society's finest. (In later years, Savannahians nicknamed his home, which was defined by wide columns on the front, "Little Tara.")

Little Gracie Watson was was loved dearly by her parents, W. J. and Frances Watson. As the only child of the luxury hoteliers, Gracie was always dressed in her Sunday best, even down to the buttons on her tiny boots.

As managers of the beloved Pulaski House, one of the city's finest hotels, the high end establishment was also a popular setting for wedding receptions, family reunions, and galas hosted by wealthy Savannahians. And it never failed: When people gathered at the Pulaski House, they always asked for Gracie.

Sometimes she hid behind her mother's skirt tail, peering out shyly with wide eyes. Other times she skipped through the lobby, her thick locks bouncing up and down in sync with her jog. Gracie was a child filled with the beauty of a foal, well-groomed, yet innocently curious. Her parents had taught her the Southern way of speaking to adults with respectful, "yes, ma'am," and "no sir," responses. In fact, she was so hospitable, return visitors were known to ask for the manner-filled Gracie when they checked in.

It was Easter week, and a hint of frost added a sparkle to Savannah's pink and purple azaleas. As so often occurs, the early frost forced the plants to bloom prematurely, much to the dismay of the town's horticulturists. Little Gracie complained of a cough, and soon her ailment escalated to severe chills and a violent fever. Savannah physicians were called to the hotel where the family resided, but just two days after Easter, little Gracie passed away from pneumonia in the weary arms of her grieving mother.

Savannahians mourned her death, and the *Savannah Morning News* eulogized Gracie in an editorial that stated, "Gracie's sweetness was abundant and flowed into the hallways and ballrooms of the city's hotel, promising cheer to every guest who checked in. Our city grieves with her parents and the angels in heaven must be adoring their new friend."

Soon after the doctor pronounced her passing, the hotel staff went to work, preparing the parlors of the hotel for Gracie's coffin and a service the next day. Townsfolk flocked to show their respects and there was standing room only in the floral-covered hotel salons as person after person sadly traipsed by the shrine dedicated to the child. As Gracie's parents succumbed to their horrendous grief, a horse and buggy laden with her tiny casket made the trek to the beautiful Bonaventure Cemetery for the burial. When the last shovel of dirt covered the grave, the family returned to the hotel, where the evening was consumed with stories of Gracie's past

Several years later, times were tough in Savannah, and a new job opportunity forced Gracie's parents to relocate to New Jersey to run a new hotel. They never returned, even in their death, leaving Gracie the sole occupant of the family plot at Bonaventure.

Walz was nearly finished with another ornate headstone. The marble piece was symbolic of life beyond this world and featured a beautiful laurel branch that enhanced the letter *H*, for the deceased. The time had finally come to etch his signature into the flat marble surface beneath the laurel branch. He completed the final touch with a strong sense of accomplishment and began to clean and organize his tools for the next job. Washing up and preparing to go to bed, he was startled by a loud knock. Disheveled and exhausted from several long days and nights of work, he drudgingly made his way down the steps from the second floor.

When he opened the door, he was met by a middle-aged man, well dressed to the very brim of his hat. The gentleman stood hesitantly on the sidewalk at the bottom of the stairs, having first knocked and then quickly descended, as he was overcome with emotion.

"What can I do for you, sir?" Walz asked, beckoning him inside.

As the man entered and Walz closed the door, he could hear thunder in the distance. Walz adjusted his dusty glasses and uttered a half-friendly greeting. And then the visitor spoke.

"Sir," the man said, "I would like to inquire about your services."

His words were choked by sadness as he struggled to speak.

Reaching into his pocket, the gentleman held up a photograph of a beautiful young girl. Walz studied the image.

"I understand. You've obviously just lost your daughter. Let's get started on this now. Tell me about your daughter," Walz said tenderly.

"Thank you."

And with that, the gentleman turned away and walked out the door and into the dark street.

Walz headed back up to the studio as lightning flashed through the staircase windows, illuminating his path. By then the storm was raging, and Walz wondered if it would distract him from his work. He hadn't met Gracie, and with only a single photograph, he was dreading the task of trying to produce her likeness in marble. Perhaps he should have declined the offer. But, on second thought, his heart empathized with this father who had just lost his daughter. So, as the rain escalated and the storm continued to pound, Walz carefully retrieved the tools that he had wrapped and stored just an hour before.

As he studied the photograph of the little girl, a massive bolt of lightning struck. Perhaps it hit his home? But Walz was so engrossed in the photograph, wondering how he could possibly bring it to life, he ignored the sound. As another clash of thunder responded with a boom so terrible that it shook the walls, Walz glanced over toward a model's chair that he kept in his studio just a few feet away. Rubbing his strained and heavy eyes, he couldn't believe what he saw.

She was sitting in the chair with her legs daintily crossed. As he stared, he suddenly realized that he was looking at the image of Gracie—an image that was alive!

"I must be dreaming," he said to himself. "I'm tired and I should rest."

But then the light inside his studio turned to dark, leaving Walz in a room that was now filled with blackness.

Then, another flash!

And suddenly, as his eyes locked on the chair, the light revealed that the little girl was still there.

Without warning, darkness came again. Walz froze to see what would occur next.

Flash!

The little girl was motioning him to pick up his instruments.

Walz obliged and began to carve her likeness from the sweet face of her image sitting there in his chair. He worked like a madman in between the darkness and light, and as the storm raged throughout the night, his work became a wild obsession. Without so much as a moment to rest his hands, he pursued the likeness of the girl with a vengeance.

The morning sunlight peered through the shutters. Gracie's father drew strength from the storm and armed with the words he couldn't speak the night before, he barged into the unlocked front door and ran up the stairs to find a tousled Walz collapsed on the floor. The model's chair sat empty. Above the unconscious artist stood a likeness of Gracie that was so true to her spirit that her father fell to his knees in disbelief, extending his arms to the daughter he once held in life. The partially finished statue was overwhelming and so true to Gracie's spirit, that her father couldn't gaze on it any longer.

Without so much as a word, he assisted the exhausted sculptor to his feet. Embracing Walz, his tears fell on the artist's dusty apron. He finally let go, turned, and fled down the staircase.

She was indeed lifelike, and her resemblance to Gracie was uncanny. Her chubby cheeks were framed by perfectly cut bangs that were thick, like her mother's. Her sweet, humble smile was complemented by a remarkably accurate rendering of her long, flowing, curly brown hair and accentuated by a deep-set dimple in her chin. She was wearing her favorite skirt, topped with a ruffled blouse with cuffed sleeves, the mark of her mother's meticulous attention to her wardrobe. Her little, boot-laden legs were in a ladylike position, as if her mother were commanding her to sit up straight and dignified. In one hand she held a rosebud, a symbol of her innocence. Her other hand rested on a small tree trunk, perhaps an illustration of her favorite place to hide. Walz spelled her name below the sculpted image in stick letters, as if Gracie had written it herself. In the moments of his passion, maybe she had carved them herself.

Mesmerized by the likeness, her awestruck father murmured, "That is Gracie."

Today Gracie watches over the butterflies and birds of Bonaventure's magnificent grounds. Those who visit her occasionally leave presents of toys, flowers, and shiny pennies. Some claim that when those gifts are moved or taken away, Gracie cries tears of blood. Others say her tears water the very ground where flowers bloom each spring.

Nearby in Section A, Lot 331, Walz is buried. Ironically, there is no headstone, just a simple wooden sign bearing his name.

A BANKER'S NIGHTMARE

Ever since the Pulaski House was bulldozed and a modern bank was built at its old location, strange findings have kept bank employees on their toes. From dungeons where slaves were kept by wealthy cotton merchants to secret underground hiding places where prostitutes sat awaiting their nightly rendezvous, grim remnants of the past remind employees that the grip of evil still has a strong hold on the site today.

It wasn't easy finding a job in banking.

The downturn of the U.S. economy and his graduation date just happened to coincide. So young Seth, a brilliant honors student who had recently completed his studies in business and finance at the University of Georgia (UGA), found himself tossed into the real world and desperately seeking employment. He was told that Savannah might be a good place to start, and after interviewing at UGA's job fair during his final semester in Athens, he had a good bite on an entry-level commercial loan trainee position.

Community Bank was what was labeled an "up and coming bank," and Seth was impressed by the promises in the career brochure that read, "We put the customer first" and "We go the extra mile so you can enjoy life." Those were just a couple of the company's philosophies listed.

Seth adored Savannah's shady squares and Community Bank opened right out onto one of the city's most pleasant spots. The shady square was adjacent to Johnson Square in the middle of the "banking district" of Savannah. He would enjoy lunchtime picnics, listen to live music on summer afternoons, and possibly even join a gym just a few blocks away. He could ride his bike to work and be within walking distance of local pubs, where he could meet friends after work. It seemed like the perfect mix for a college grad's first job out of school.

Savannah would provide the picture-perfect setting for his first adventure in banking, and a job here was a great reward for four years of studying business.

There had been some turnover at Community Bank, but Seth wasn't going to let that hinder his opportunity. He had heard from "sources" that something strange was keeping the staff spinning. But Seth didn't care. He signed on the dotted line and called home to proclaim that he was now a full-time employed citizen of Savannah and officially off his dad's payroll.

It was his first workday morning, and after a quick run, Seth charged into the local coffee shop, grabbed a cup of coffee, and headed back to his loft apartment for a shower. After unwrapping the Hartmann briefcase his mother had given him for graduation, he adjusted his tie, looked himself squarely in the eye, hopped on his bike, and headed to his first day on the job.

"Welcome to the banking world, Seth," his manager, a tall slender woman named Beth, said with a typical Savannah drawl. "We ah so glad to have you he-ah," she continued, dragging her words into multisyllabic sounds as Seth smiled, silently amused. As they reviewed the typical first-day checklist, she paused and placed her slender white fingers on Seth's hand. Her lips were bright, glossy red; he could almost see his reflection in the shimmer. He thought it was odd that a manager would treat a new employee with such a lack of professionalism. He was also wondering why this woman was so pale and, on top of that, wore a lipstick color that almost looked vampirish. But Seth shook it off as just a simple case of Southern hospitality with a dose of glamour.

"This is a truly graaaa-nnnd place to work, but I must warn you," she said. "We think our building is inhabited."

"Inhabited?"

Seth tried to comprehend the definition of the word and realized that UGA's business professors had taught him absolutely nothing about "inhabitants." Quickly shaking off the awkward silence that followed, he laughed, "Oh, don't worry. I'm not afraid of ghosts."

The bank was situated in a four-story building at the corner of Bull and West Bryan Streets in Savannah on what was once the site of a posh hotel with magnificent views of the city's flourishing Johnson Square. With palm trees framing one side of the exterior and an awning-covered bellman's stand ready to greet wealthy guests, the Pulaski House was one of three of the grandest places to stay in Savannah from the 1800s through 1956, when it was demolished. Built in 1838 by Peter Wiltberger, it was described by one newspaper writer as "one of the finest hotels in the South—with cuisine not excelled outside of New York."

With "special weekly rates" advertised on a postcard, Savannah's "newest and oldest" hotel offered single rooms for $1.00 and double rooms for $1.50. The parlors were decorated with flamboyant furnishings, designed by New York-ers, making the hotel the perfect venue for large wedding receptions and social gatherings for local and visiting aristocrats. Among the hotel's guests (claimed) were General Robert E. Lee and Governor Joseph Brown. Jefferson Davis was taken to the hotel after he was captured at Louisville, Georgia, following the crumbling of the Confederacy. It was there that he and Mrs. Davis stayed until Jefferson was imprisoned in a Virginia fort for many months. In later years a newspaper article captured the scope of the impressive list of guests who graced the halls of the Pulaski House:

> *During this period it was the day when Savannah was great in the world's cotton business, the busy harbor, the business section, the Customs House and other vital elements of the city's business and social life were hardly more than the proverbial stone's throw distance. There were many distinguished men, no doubt, who paid the hotel—and some of its maidservants—a visit.*

W. J. and Frances Watson ran and lived at the Pulaski House during the first part of their careers managing hotels. And sadly, the hotel was the setting for the somber funeral services of their six-year-old daughter, Gracie, who died of pneumonia in 1889.

If walls could talk, this building would possibly top the list for literally hundreds of scandalous tales of infidelity, joy, and scandal.

On October 13, 1907, the announcement was made that the hotel was to be remodeled under the new proprietorship of "Messrs. Stubbs & Keen," according to an article in the *Savannah Morning News*. The work would be "in accordance with the plans prepared by Architect Percy Sugden and under his supervision."

According to these plans, the courtyard at the rear of the building would be enclosed and converted into a poolroom. There would be eight tables and additional toilets installed "with special provisions for cleanliness and ventilation." The poolroom would be finished "in weathered oak with steel ceiling and would be well lighted from above." The lobby would undergo a complete renovation, new glass would be installed in the front entrance, and the floors of the new poolroom and bathrooms would be "laid with a monolith finish known as the Puritan sanitary floor" and would present a "rich and cheerful appearance on entering the hotel."

In addition, eighteen rooms would be constructed with private bathrooms, and steam heating would be installed throughout the building. The article concluded by saying that the new owners were committed to making their facility "in the class of modern motels."

The Pulaski House and its proprietors enjoyed fifty more years of prosperity until plans were announced that the hotel would be torn down and replaced by a "modern office," and later, a cafeteria. Little did the contractors realize that what lay beneath the facade of the aging structure would be both evil and disturbing.

So, in January of 1956, the old cage elevator fell to the hands of the "welder's torch." Bricks began "sliding down wooden chutes and were slowly taken away by Negro workers," according to newspaper reports.

As brochures depicting the lavish parties held at the old hotel were uncovered, workers continued dismantling the structure, finding even more hidden secrets. Among them was the announcement of an event to "entertain guests in elegant surroundings when Texas was still a part of Mexico . . . in 1828 . . . and 33 years before the War Between the States." As the workers delved deeper, they reached the street level, where they came upon a "heavy mesh wire fastened beneath one of the basement windows" that led to a dark, moldy dungeon.

It was that dungeon that perhaps held clues to the strange happenings that would occur years later when the site was cleared and repurposed to house restaurants and, finally, a bank. Indeed, the findings were astounding.

The newspaper reported, "Underneath the building, there can be seen today, a series of bricked-in cells. These are the dungeon chambers with a bricked-up fireplace of massive size in one such chamber. Some of them run up to the edge of the pavement and are discernable through the iron grating that makes up part of the sidewalk." The article proceeded to say that the dungeons held the slaves belonging to the "rich traders from the North who came south in the winter or the wealthy rice planters from the vicinity of Savannah who passed through enroute North."

With those findings came theories about ghostly encounters. Was there a passageway that linked the dungeon to an underground tunnel leading to the river? Workers discovered artifacts that led to some answers, including a porcelain-topped cuspidor of the type used by the wealthy found in the dungeon. Could this place be a place filled with sordid tales of Savannah's wealthy and prominent businessmen conducting indiscretions with prostitutes?

When the new, modern office building replaced the old hotel in the 1960s, a cafeteria was opened on the ground floor. For several years, strange happenings kept hungry diners and cafeteria employees on their toes. Women who visited the restrooms and placed their pocketbooks on the floor would have their purses snatched from beneath the stall door. Once they exited the stall to retrieve their purses, they would find them turned over with the contents emptied and items like red lipstick and nail polish strewn about. Nothing was stolen from the purses, and it appeared that whoever/whatever was grabbing them was doing it just for entertainment. They reported these strange happenings to the management and after investigation, there were no conclusions.

Could the ghost, or ghosts, invading the women's restrooms be little Gracie, who was a former resident of the hotel and died there? After all, her parents did run the place. Or could it be the work of slaves who were once imprisoned in the dungeon of the old Pulaski House? Perhaps they were seeking things of value to exchange for their freedom or revenge on those who placed them under lock and chain. Could these be the spirits of the women of ill repute who were hidden beneath the structure, still desiring cosmetics to keep them beautiful?

Seth had read all about the hotel's history, but today all he could think of was his new job and about how quickly the hours were going by.

It was difficult to believe that on his second day of employment, he would be allowed into the bank's vault that was situated beneath the ground level in a basement-type room. When a customer came in holding an envelope full of jewels and asked for his help in opening a safe deposit box, he, being the only one available to assist her, took care of the paperwork and issued the key to her. When he turned to the next cubicle seeking Beth's nod of approval, he discovered her desk was cleared and an empty chair was turned around backward, facing the square. Maybe she was ill and had left early? Or maybe she had gone to lunch?

As Seth ushered the customer to the elevator and down to the vault, he could hear the distinct sound of a woman laughing and a conversation that was laced with scandal. The laugh sounded familiar. Intermingled with it he heard, "Stop it! You're making me laugh. We must hurry. Your wife will be looking for you soon."

Closing the vault behind him, Seth ushered the client out the door. He then approached a young teller who was also a recent college grad.

"Where's Beth?" he asked. "I heard a woman's voice laughing below when I took that lady down to the vault where the safe deposit boxes are. It's really creepy down there. Do you know where Beth is?"

Glancing back toward his desk, he noticed that his new Hartmann briefcase was missing. He then turned to the teller as an icy revelation struck him like a wild dream in a dead sleep. Distracted by a walk-in customer, the teller politely completed the transition and leaned over the counter, connecting with Seth's eyes.

"Beth who?"

Seth spun around and headed straight to his desk. This time, the briefcase was lying open on his desk. As he grabbed the handle and attempted to close it, he noticed something inside: an opened and half-used tube of red lipstick.

Had he encountered a ghost from the cellar below?

Was his interaction with Beth something that had actually happened or was he going crazy? No one would believe his theories, especially his landlord when he attempted to break the lease he had just signed. His dad would never believe him either.

As he raced across the square, he could only conclude that fate led him to a mysterious encounter with the past. He had been lured by the spirit of a women who perhaps, resided in a dungeon below the bank. Nothing would persuade him to return to the building at Bull and West Bryant Street.

THE OLDE PINK HOUSE

The Olde Pink House has become one of Savannah's most iconic pleasantries. Noted for its distinct pink color, it looks out over the square where the statue of John Wesley, the founder of Methodism, oversees an astoundingly beautiful canopy of hundred-year oak trees and quaint park benches. If you venture in on a cold, windy night and the fires are burning in the Pink House's downstairs tavern called Planters, you just might encounter a surprising ghost undiscovered except in the digital images captured found on your mobile phone.

Mark and Dawn were looking forward to their return trip to Savannah. Celebrating their fifth anniversary in the city where they had wed would be extra special if they could get a reservation at their favorite restaurant, The Olde Pink House. When they called, a friendly voice picked up the line:

"Hello. Thank you for calling The Olde Pink House. This is Blanche. How may I assist?"

Blanche, the restaurant's event planner, was celebrating a milestone herself. The call would be the first one on the anniversary of the day, eight years previous, she started working at the famous Savannah landmark.

"We look forward to seeing you tonight," she told Mark. "I'll reserve your favorite table in the tavern and make sure the candlelight is glowing!"

As Mark and Dawn spent the afternoon touring the city by carriage, Blanche, accompanied by her four-year-old son, Pearson, worked downstairs in the restaurant's office scheduling deliveries and booking group reservations. It was the first day of Tybee Island's Pirate Fest, an annual four-day celebration that she and her son attended each year on her day off. In honor of the festival, they were both dressed in pirate attire. Although she would have to work that evening, they decided to dress up anyway—after all, pirates were a part of their lives on Tybee Island where they lived.

"Pow, bam, die, you matey," said Pearson, who appeared to be swatting someone in his mom's office.

"What are you doing, Pearson?" Blanche asked.

He kept on swinging and mumbling words she couldn't understand, until he finally replied, "Oh, I'm just killing off the ghosts of pirates with my guns, Mommy. They are in your office."

Pearson's imagination was at work, and Blanche was thankful that he could entertain himself with his imaginary friends as she continued plowing through the paperwork. It was getting late, and soon his father would arrive to pick him up for the night. She thought nothing about their conversation, at least not until later.

Tourists often stood in the square to take photos of the beautiful Pink House as a backdrop. Next door at the Planters Inn, Mark and Dawn were checking into their room. Soon they would be spending a cozy evening in the dimly lit cellar where wine bottles are stored in an old bank vault.

The couple emerged from the front door of the inn and headed up the stairs to the restaurant, heeding the Careful warning posted on the steep front staircase. They grasped the rail, taking the stone steps in stride like rock climbers. Peering inside, they were greeted by a hostess standing next to a portrait of the grand and distinguished, James Habersham, former owner of the home that he had built and lived in during the 1700s.

"Hello, James," said Mark, addressing the portrait. "We're baaaaaack!"

Habersham's bright eyes appeared to be looking directly into theirs, and his chubby cheeks and elongated face seemed flushed, as if he had rushed about prior to sitting for the portrait. His whimsical expression boasted mischief, and Mark and Dawn always enjoyed his "many looks" when they returned for a visit.

"Mr. Habersham has been looking for you two," the hostess quipped. Around the corner, Blanche appeared, greeting the two like long-lost friends.

"It's great to see you. Let me tell you some of the weird things that have been happening in this restaurant," she said, standing tall in her black boots and pirate gear.

Tales upon tales advise that Mr. Habersham is, indeed, present in the place where he allegedly hung himself, distraught over the death of his wife. Doors close and lock. Candles refuse to stay lit. Skewed tableware is neatly set within seconds of a server's departure. Freezing orbs touch guests on the arms and neck. Pirates walk through brick walls and into others. Drink glasses shatter and fly off the shelves. This is The Olde Pink House where evil is present in the form of friendly and unassuming ghosts who are apparently amused by their own taunting of the guests.

It was 1738 when James Habersham first graced the shores of what is now called Savannah. Asked by his close friend, the famed evangelist George Whitefield, to accompany him to the port city, he was excited about venturing to the new colony. Habersham was a teacher and Whitefield was the first supervisor of the Bethesda Orphanage. Habersham was also engaged in the shipping of supplies from Charleston, which eventually led to his becoming one of the most successful shipping entrepreneurs of his time.

Habersham soon acquired land for growing rice and eventually owned more than fifteen thousand acres at his peak. His interest was swayed toward politics, and he became a senior counselor and later council president and acting governor of Georgia. With three sons who were all highly successful, Habersham's life was indeed well-rounded and accomplished.

His wealth was evident throughout the historic structure, with extravagant details in every room, and his presence was still palpable. The parlor to the left of the hostess station offered a lovely view of the square, and a mantel where Habersham himself snuffed out the candles. Spooking all who watched the flames dance and then disappear, his ritual was like a choreographed special effect. To the right of the hostess station, at the far end of the home, stands the original vault belonging to a bank that once occupied the structure. Upstairs, the bedrooms have been transformed into intimate gathering places for diners who partake of the scenic views of the square, where the statue stands. Guests dining upstairs have reported seeing Habersham stroll through the room in full military garb.

Blanche ushered them down the stairs and into the tavern below, where she sat them at a table in the glow of the massive fireplace. Although absorbed in the aesthetics of the mansion, Blanche's intriguing tales, and the beauty of the moment, the couples' appetites were growing. After all, wasn't there to converse about ghosts. They were already familiar with the restaurant's history.

With the exterior color of the building a bit of a mystery in itself, The Olde Pink House at 23 Abercorn Street was a constant source of interest to ghost hunters. Throughout the seasons of the city, their mission is to prove the spirits are plentiful in the popular establishment. With their technology, they look beyond the red clay bricks that have bled through the stucco to create "a pink house," and more deeply into the realm of the spiritual world. Perhaps that is what attracted the couple to the Pink House in the first place—the stories, plus the fresh crispy scored flounder and crème brûlée.

Their table was in the very center of the rustic room, between two magnificent brick hearths with fires blazing. The dark oak ceiling beams added to the rustic atmosphere, and with a pianist playing softly as they dined, the couple was indeed mesmerized by the charm of this Savannah favorite.

As they settled into their red velvet chairs, Blanche offered to take a photo to commemorate the evening. Mark, standing behind Dawn, held a glass up as if to make a toast, and they both smiled as Blanche snapped the photo. With the appetizers already delivered to the table, they opted to tuck their mobile phones away and enjoy every morsel of the meal they had waited for months to devour.

The ghost of James Habersham is a "neat freak," according to the Pink House employees who are familiar with his habits. He often straightens out tables that are in disarray, handling what the busboys call "a work in progress."

At times he pulls the restroom doors tightly shut, trapping guests inside. Occasionally, it is the ghost of Habersham who raises floor planks in the tavern, causing servers to trip.

But tonight was all about Mark and Dawn, and no ghost was going to change that.

The couple had already experienced his antics. During a previous visit, Dawn left her dinner setting in disarray while she made a quick trip to the restroom. When she didn't return, Mark called for the manager, and as happens so frequently, Dawn was locked in the small, but beautiful, restroom.

Tonight, they felt, the spirits were at rest.

When the final spoonful of dessert was finished, Mark and Dawn realized they were the only ones left in the tavern. The evening had been uneventful, just as they had requested. It was a cold weekday night, and Savannahians rarely ventured out late when winter burst its chill through the thick branches of live oaks.

"It's great that we're staying right next door," Mark said. "It's not far, and I'm so full. I'm glad our walk will be brief."

They paid their bill, handwrote a thank-you note to their hostess, bid the bartender farewell, and exited the tavern.

A few minutes later, the silence of the restaurant's cleanup staff was broken.

The bartender was wiping down the wooden bar for the last time when a loud banging sent him rushing to the door. When he opened it, Mark was standing there with a distressed look on his face.

"Is Blanche still here?" he asked. "I need to speak to her right away."

"Yes, sir. I'll get her," the bartender replied.

Skipping down the stairs in her black-laced boots and pirate's vest, and smiling as if it were her first hour at work, Blanche reached out to shake Mark's hand. Instead, he placed his mobile phone in her hand. It had been a stressful night for her, with two of the waitstaff out, wine spilled at table eight, multiple complaints about the lights going out in the restroom, and a cold draft sending one diner back to his car to retrieve a coat. If ever there were a night for the spirits to show themselves, this would be it.

"There's a ghost in our picture," Mark said, nervously. "Look."

And with that, Blanche froze.

There, behind Mark and Dawn in the photo she had snapped herself, was the clear face of James Habersham himself, floating in the round mirror behind them. A ring of what appeared to be smoke curled around the back of the couple's heads, forming the his facial features. There in the glass they were holding up in a toast was a perfect image of his chubby cheeks, formed in the light reflecting into the goblet.

Blanche squealed "Oh my!" as she recalled her son's antics along with his comments that afternoon in the office. His words resounded in her soul.

"Mom, I'm killing ghosts of a man and pirates with my guns..."

Mark and Dawn left for home the next day with chilling memories on a photo they would never delete. Yes, they had encountered a strange guest that showed up that evening at The Olde Pink House. Blanche continues to work there, tending to the details that keep The Olde Pink House among the most beloved restaurants in the South. She states that since that night, she does not work alone. After viewing the photograph, she said, "Things just started opening up." Feeling as though spirits surround her as she works, Blanche said, "Every once in a while I will come close to falling and something, or someone, will keep me on my feet."

"I think he's a good spirit," she continued, "and he looks after me because I take care of the house. He cares for me." Whispering, she went on to say that she believes that somewhere beneath the heart-pine floors of the tavern is a chest filled with pirate's gold, and that Habersham always enjoys being around a crowd of hungry diners.

Each day, the lines start to form on the sidewalk at 5 p.m. as The Tavern at The Olde Pink House opens for happy hour. As the guests enter, the eyes of Mr. Habersham never miss casting a glance down as they are received. And as dusk settles just outside and through the window of the living room, one by one, the lit candles flicker and then silently, become more faint until they finally go out.

Some things never change.

BROUGHTON AND BULL

Imagine this: Italian cuisine in Savannah, Georgia.

It was a crazy idea for the 1990s, but Savannahians who knew entrepreneur Adriano Lanz understood that he was all about perfection. Transforming a former Lerner's department store on Savannah's fledgling Broughton Street into a first-class restaurant would require significant capital, but with Lanz at the helm, his vision and focus would inspire the architects to design something eye-catching and classy that would attract Savannah's wealthiest clientele.

With enormous windows that looked out onto Savannah's bustling downtown, and a contemporary interior of cool tiles and hardwood accents, guests not only dined there, but also enjoyed a comfortable and trendy wine bar that also faced Broughton Street. And just as Lanz excelled in the aesthetics, he also successfully engaged a first-class chef along with a well-trained and detail-oriented staff.

When the doors of Il Pasticcio opened, Savannah's finest were drawn to its contemporary style and big-city feel, and soon the restaurant became the town's most talked-about place to dine. But it wasn't just Savannahians who turned Italian. This establishment earned a reputation of one of the country's best and here's how they achieved this.

Billed as a "metropolitan dining experience," Lanz's restaurant, which opened in 1993, endured a run of more than seventeen years. He proudly voiced his recipe for success in ads that read, "When you walk in here, it's like a Broadway show. We're performing for the people. It's not just about the food experience—everything must synchronize. The hostesses, the bartenders, the services, the managers, are all a part of it. If customers leave and say it was just OK, then we failed in one of those areas."

As more and more Savannahians became regulars, it seemed that Lanz was doing what many had wished for—putting Savannah's modest Broughton Street on the pages of national and international publications—and making a name for himself and his city in the process.

John was a student at the Savannah College of Art and Design, seeking a managerial job that would give him night hours while he attended class during the day. Moving to Savannah from Baltimore to attend the highly acclaimed art school posed a financial challenge for his parents, and he promised his dad that he would help with the expenses by taking a part-time job. With a flair for interior design and a hidden desire to venture into the culinary world, John found a mentor when he met Adriano Lanz.

The two hit it off right away, and nothing pleased Lanz more than to adopt yet another apprentice. John felt good about working in a place where he could learn the business and still have a few hours of study time each day.

Starting as a waiter, he soon learned to recite the menu (which was mostly Italian) and to comprehend all the ingredients in the expansive lists of entrees and appetizers. Locals began to ask for him by name, and soon he was promoted to assistant manager.

All seemed to be going well. John was learning the business, and Lanz was able to trust him with important tasks. But there was something lurking, something disturbingly evil that was never brought up in John's daily conferences with Lanz. The young man from Baltimore was about to encounter a task that wasn't written in his job description.

John had been on the job for two months, and things appeared to be running smoothly. But behind the scenes and within the walls of the upstairs office, something was secretly tormenting him, and it was something that he would never share with his boss. Each night, he just sat back and watched the nightmare unfold.

One evening after closing, John was busy preparing to lock up. The bells of the Cathedral of St. John the Baptist had just chimed when he turned the key to secure the front door of the restaurant. It was nearly 1:00 a.m., and there were few people still out on Broughton Street. Extremely cautious as he carried the evening's cash pouch beneath his shirt as he locked up inside, John had only one regret: He wished he had learned to carry and shoot a gun. But for now, his nightly duties of counting the cash and closing out the day would be accomplished alone and without fear. After all, everyone had left. He was inside and safe.

John entered the office, settled into his chair, and began moving the paperwork to the sides of the desk to clear a work space. Although closing up was a task he enjoyed, he also felt that he was developing what people in this part of the country call "the creeps."

There were no windows in the office he shared with Lanz. Perhaps that is why the owner spent little time there. The room was always cold, and there was no explanation for its frigid atmosphere. The door was solid metal with a deadbolt, and at times John felt as though he were in a meat locker or enclosed in a pantry as he counted the money and tallied up the figures for the day.

"Eric Clapton," he thought. "I'll put on some Eric Clapton to help fill the sound void and maybe speed up the task." Scrolling through the music stored on his computer, he hit PLAY. Nothing happened. Too tired to check the connections, he opted to skip it.

By then it was 2:00 a.m., and he could hear the church bells once more. Picking up the phone to dial his girlfriend, Jina, he heard a very loud banging sound coming from the staircase. His heart beating vigorously, he hung up the phone and got up, bravely opened the door, and called out.

"Is anyone there? . . . Frank, that's not funny. . . . Stop it. . . . Frank?"

The banging continued. Leery of pranks, he decided to pack up and get out as quickly as he could.

No one would believe him if he shared his fears with coworkers, and he was not about to act as though it bothered him. It was probably just a bad joke.

The next night the restaurant hosted a private party, and the guests gathered for the cocktail hour around six. John, attentive as always, suspected that someone on the staff was watching him as he greeted the guests, so he mentioned the previous night's activities to no one. Dressed in a starched white shirt and black bow tie, he looked crisp and professional. The event brought in well-known Savannahians, and when it ended, John unbuttoned his shirt, released his tie, and, wearing a T-shirt and his black dress pants, headed upstairs.

The party ended around 11:00 p.m., and with only a few tips and a single check to cover the night's activities, closing out wouldn't take him long. This time, John was convinced that there was no one else in the building, as he had ventured into the kitchen, the alley outside, and even the restrooms.

Just as he emptied the cash bag out on the desk, the banging started. It was almost as if someone were beating two metal trashcan lids together, but this time it grew louder as each minute passed. There, in the room that he was now calling his "shelter," the only thing separating him from this frightening noise happened to be the only door he could use to retreat. Feeling a combination of annoyance and fear, he left all the money spread out on the desk, grabbed his coat, and raced down the stairs and out the front door. His task would have to wait.

The next morning, even though it was his night off, John called just as he woke up and arranged a meeting with his boss. He told Lanz that he would be happy to close the restaurant the following night, but he would like to assume new duties after that. He couldn't bring himself to tell Lanz that he was afraid to be alone in the office they shared.

That evening, when the final guests left and the kitchen crew exited, John climbed the stairs to the office and bolted the door. Within five minutes, the sounds began.

John picked up the phone and started dialing his girlfriend, Jina.

"Hey! I'm afraid. You know I told you something creepy happened last night here at the restaurant? Well, it's happening again," he said.

The moment Jina had answered her phone, the clanging had stopped. John was beginning to feel as though he shouldn't have bothered calling her. Was he going mad? Was he going to look foolish by calling her again?

Looking around the room, it appeared calm and serene, the perfect atmosphere for catching up on paperwork. And the best part was that there was no more banging.

It was quiet. Dead quiet.

"Hold on a minute. I'll be right back."

And with that, John opened the door, stood on the staircase, and listened intently. Nothing. Silence.

"OK, I'm back," he said. "You still there?"

Several seconds ticked by before he heard his girlfriend's voice.

Almost speaking over him, Jina said, "Hey, John. I can hardly hear you. What's that loud banging noise?"

"Dear Mr. Lanz," his letter read. "Due to personal reasons, tonight will be my last night working here. Thank you for the opportunity and best regards."

John licked the envelope and left it on the desk. As he walked out, he overheard his boss whispering to the chef.

"I've lost another manager. I believe this building is possessed."

THE SPIRITS OF GRAYSON STADIUM

Savannah's minor-league stadium has hosted some of the greats in baseball history. From Babe Ruth to Mickey Mantle, they've all experienced the action in the place that is filled with nostalgia and promises of fame. For one young umpire in the 1920s, Savannah's stadium was magical—until a play at home changed the course of a game and may have cost him his life.

Working for Savannah's minor-league baseball team could be a dream job unless you happen to be the one in charge of locking up the stadium. That chore was one that no employee would volunteer to handle. But Mark didn't mind. He was a fast runner, and he had developed a flair for getting the job done efficiently. His strategy? Wear good running shoes and don a headset. Doing so would block out the the crackling and creaking sounds that greeted him at the end of every game night after the crowds had emptied the parking lots. He could use his swift feet to get him to his car and quickly away from the sobs and mysterious footsteps that he often heard coming from Savannah's home-team locker room.

As the team's media manager, Mark was in charge of public relations for the Sand Gnats. Savannahians had grown accustomed to the name given to the minor league team in the 1990s by their owners, the world-famous Los Angeles Dodgers. Mark's job was to see that the stands were filled with fans on hot summer nights. He was the creativity behind the team, and he took great pleasure in delivering round after round of ways to attract people to the stadium. There were "Thirsty Thursdays," where patrons could drink beer at reduced prices, and "T-Shirt Nights," where the first thousand fans entering the stadium would receive a free Sand Gnats shirt. Few were the nights when Mark failed to come up with a way to lure fans to the park.

During the day, he was willing to help out in most every way. If the programs were ready to be picked up, Mark would volunteer. He would inspect the vendors' booths, and he would even work the sales station for Sand Gnat gear. But there was one area where he refused the challenge: His job description didn't say anything about communicating with the supernatural.

Built in 1926, Grayson Stadium, as it was renamed after originally being called Municipal Stadium, has avoided modernization and remains one of the country's oldest and most nostalgic ballparks. While there are signs of aging, improvements through the years have been subtle enough to spare the stadium of changes that would distract from its charm. You can still get giant boiled peanuts there, and the kosher hot dogs are juicy and delicious. Kids still clamor for players' autographs long after the game has ended, and adults still drown themselves in frosty soft drinks and ice-cold beer.

The original wooden bleachers have been repainted a blinding primary blue, but if you look closely, you'll see the crackly surfaces peeling, revealing the years layers of paint that have been plastered and repainted over and over again. The scorekeeper (a youthful and athletic teenager who, using a ladder, once hung the numbers) has been replaced by a flashy digital screen, but other than a new office for the staff and air-conditioning for the press box, most things remain the same, including the locker rooms with their concrete walls that have been painted over several times.

As with most nostalgic stadiums, there are some obvious scars prevalent in the building's aesthetics. A hurricane destroyed a major part of the stadium in 1940, and the following year a construction project for improvements was halted by the war. There are still signs where the brickwork is unfinished. The city of Savannah has opted to leave those flaws as they are, a reminder of the sacrifices made during wartime.

Mark could endure working in a strange environment in return for a good, steady job. These were tough economic times and, as far as he was concerned, the voices, sobbing, and shuffling from the locker room after hours could continue. He would carry out his duties in season or out. Granted, there were plenty of times when he was afraid, but the ghost in the locker room didn't seem to be going anywhere.

The organization hadn't kept accurate records through the years, and no matter how much Mark delved, he couldn't figure out why the shadow of sadness within those walls lingered. He finally gave up guessing. There wasn't enough research available to explain whose tears were flowing there after he turned the lights off and sealed the door. Sadly, it would be something that he might never learn.

Jack Rogers needed money.

The twenty-six-year-old Citadel graduate had served his stint in the army and wound up back in Charleston, South Carolina, where his wife, Lillee, was pregnant with their first child. As a former baseball standout both at Charleston High School and in college, he was the perfect candidate for umpires' school. Fit and trim, he would take on the boys of summer in the newly formed South Atlantic League and try to earn a decent living umpiring games by night and pumping gas at Henry's Gas Station on Tradd Street in downtown Charleston by day.

Baseball was Rogers's passion. He loved both watching and playing the game. And he loved standing in the center of all the action as an umpire. After all, it was a relatively clean job and much less taxing on his body. He was at his best behind home plate, calling plays with the finesse of a conductor leading his orchestra. Perhaps he was lured by the scent of freshly mowed grass that enveloped the ballpark like a sumptuous haze. For Rogers, there was no finer place in the world to spend summers than on a baseball field, especially in Savannah, where the action was way hotter than on the Charleston sandlot where he played stickball as a child.

It was March of 1927 and, at Municipal Stadium (now known as Grayson), Savannahians of all ages lined up to see the game of a lifetime in a ballpark that was otherwise built for the minor leagues. In celebration of the stadium's first year as the home base for the Savannah Indians, a blockbuster major-league exhibition game was scheduled to kick off the minor-league season. The game was expected to attract fans from all across Georgia and South Carolina and would feature the 1926 World Champions, the St. Louis Cardinals, versus the New York Yankees, a team that had just won the American League pennant.

Rogers received his schedule for the season, and Savannah's exhibition game was the headlining opener. Overwhelmed by the opportunity to see some of baseball's elite players, he packed his gear, headed for the train station in Charleston, and hopped aboard the southbound for Savannah.

He could hardly believe it! He was going to umpire the Series-winning Cardinals and the New York Yankees. Playing for the Yankees that evening would be two players who were expected to draw the most attention: a young fellow named Lou Gehrig and a pudgy power hitter named Babe Ruth.

Crowds began to fill the stands as early as 2:00 p.m. Vendors sloshing beer and cold drinks made their way up and down the dark blue bleachers. Little League teams dressed in uniform headed into the right-field stands with gloves, hoping to catch fly balls, while fat men clad in Savannah Indian T-shirts waddled to their seats as cold beer slashed over the cup rims and onto the feet of those already sitting. As the sun began to set behind the scoreboard, its rays illuminated the thick, puffy clouds in the field's background, painting the landscape with hints of pink and gold.

"Oh, yeah," Rogers thought. "It was worth the sweltering train ride."

"All rise for the National Anthem," said the announcer. Rogers, with hand over heart, stood along the baseline between the two teams. He had never felt such pride as he did that very moment standing amid the greats of baseball on a perfectly beautiful evening. He wished Lillee could be there, but soon refocused on his duties as the players headed for the dugout.

As Rogers swept off home plate, the lights kicked on and, in his most assertive voice, he yelled out the words "Play ball!" followed by "Batter up!" The crowd's chants flowed like the sea on Tybee Island's shores.

On that single night, baseball in Savannah, Georgia, was electric!

Time flew and before he realized it, Jack Rogers was calling his eighth inning in a major-league game. The Cardinals were ahead 15 to 8, and with the Yankees still at bat, Babe Ruth stepped up with two outs. Ruth was already a hero. He had broken his own home run records at least three times since his first year playing in the major leagues in 1914. Exhibition game or not, he was out for blood, and the fans longed to see him hit a homer. Kids stood, gloved hands raised. Moms and dads focused on the pitcher as their baseball hero stepped up to the plate. The fat men rose from their seats, and the church groups that had driven for hours to see the game said silent prayers that Ruth would hit a homer.

"Steeeeeeeee-rike!"

Rogers called strike one on a curveball that Ruth let pass by him.

"Ball."

The fans were hardly breathing, and the kids were chomping with fury on bubble gum that had lost its flavor innings ago.

"Ball two."

The third pitch was a definitive ball, and Rogers shook off the crowd's admonishment.

Tightening his belt, Rogers's eyes met those of the Cardinals' pitcher with such intent focus that it became a distraction. The pitcher released the ball, and as it came right toward him, Ruth swung so hard that he nearly broke the bat.

Around the bases he ran, and as he passed third, the crowd seemed to flow onto the field, gleefully cheering his name.

As Ruth slid into home, Rogers, in a mighty wail, said the words that will forever haunt Savannah's stadium: "Youuuu'rrrrre out!"

Boos filled the air, and everything from shoes to programs were tossed out onto the field. Rogers had called one of the greatest players to ever play the game out, without so much as a pause. And the worst part of all, he wasn't really sure whether Ruth was really out or not.

He felt terrible.

The Cardinals went on to win the game 20 to 10. Babe Ruth went 2 for 5. It proved to be one of the worst games of his career.

As Rogers made his way into the locker room to shower after the game ended, he was greeted by angry kids, along with their parents, their friends, and their coworkers. While the winning team quickly gathered their equipment and exited, Rogers lingered inside the dark and moldy room, hoping the stadium would empty quickly.

Although the train back to Charleston didn't leave until the following morning, Rogers believed his career and reputation would be scarred for calling Babe Ruth out at home on a play that could never be replayed. He decided to stay at the stadium in the privacy and solitude of the empty locker room, and hitch a ride to the train station the next morning. That way, he wouldn't have to face his foes.

That night, as he sat on a wooden bench in the dark, Rogers made a pact with himself. If he could somehow get out of Savannah without anyone recognizing him, he would never watch, play, or umpire another game of baseball.

The 8:00 a.m. train for Charleston pulled into the Savannah station, and a crowd of about thirty travelers going north climbed aboard. After the conductor called one last "All aboard!" the doors closed, and the train slowly chugged out of the station.

Jack Rogers never boarded that train. His wife waited at the Charleston station until the last passenger exited and contacted law enforcement immediately after she presumed him missing. The local media picked up on the mystery in the next day's headline, "Umpire reported missing."

As for Mark and his communications job with the Sand Gnats, he continued to volunteer to lock up the stadium in spite of a series of events that would have sent most people running for a less stressful career.

For years Rogers's presence had been revealed in subtle, and at times annoying, ways. They were the umpire's means of revenge for the torture he received from the throngs of angry Savannah fans.

At first the problems were bothersome but insignificant. There was the season when all the tickets were printed with the correct dates, but the corresponding days of the week were wrong. When no one owned up to the mistake, all fingers pointed to Rogers. There were stadium lights that flickered whenever the team was aiming for a comeback.

One early spring game, the team's organist seemed dazed and confused during a Braves minor-league game. There in front of more than three thousand fans, she gave up playing halfway through the revered National Anthem.

One of the players found a program from the Cardinals/Yankees game crumpled up stuck between the bricks of the dugout. Equipment was found missing from the team's locker room after it had been counted. And one evening, a tired Savannah team physician found the door "stuck," and it would not open when he tried to exit.

But most disturbing of all were the sounds of a sobbing man that came from the home-team locker room long after the crowds and players had gone home.

The Sand Gnats had gone through many changes through the years, and there were few records for Mark to investigate. Those that he did find did not decisively show any strange events that could have led up to the oddities he was experiencing.

The team switched ownership several times. From the Cardinals to the Dodgers to the Rangers and finally to the Mets, Savannah's team had changed hands so many times, records were misplaced. Today, Grayson Stadium is adorned in bananas—a team, that is. The Savannah Bananas have finally brought life to the stadium for the ghost of a beleaguered umpire. It's baseball, but not really baseball. With dancing grandmas, high-stepping players, horn-tooting bands and an all-inclusive ticket that's all you can eat, the ghost has been joyfully called out with few paranormal sightings left.

Rogers's locker room descendants believe that the ghost of Grayson Stadium is, in fact, Jack Rogers, the umpire who ruled the greatest player to ever play the game out at home.

It was the disappointment of a lifetime for too many people who had come from near and far to see history made that evening in Savannah. As for Babe Ruth, after he was called out in the worst game of his career, he went on to hit sixty home runs in the same season he had played his exhibition game at Grayson Stadium.

But what happened to Rogers? If you visit the stadium, stick around after the game. Wait until the lights are turned out and listen outside the door of the home team's locker room.

Just don't be the last one to lock up.

SHIPWRECK

On hot summer weekends, thousands of tourists dot the sand and catch rays on one of the South's most hidden treasures, Tybee Island. Called "quirky" by some, Tybee is a mecca for Georgians who savor the beach's rustic allure. In the winter and spring, there are parts of the strand that are literally desolate . . . except for those spirits who were buried at sea and stirred by the greed of humanity.

It was spring break, and Addy and her roommate, Lauren, were pretending it was summer. It's a common practice among college students from Savannah who are not among the privileged who travel to exotic islands like their peers.

Addy had lived in Savannah all her life and was struggling to get through the financial burdens of college, which she was paying for herself. She would be spending spring break at home and had invited Lauren to join her. Their sorority sisters were heading down to Florida's Gulf coast, where it was much warmer and where they would have their pick of boys from the North.

Although it wasn't Florida and they were in Savannah, the girls could quickly hop in their 2014 Toyota, drop the windows and in ten minutes, get to a beach via a road that skimmed the salt marshes for several miles. Tybee Island, their picturesque and quaint getaway, was just seventeen miles east of downtown, and it had all the makings of a perfect escape from the classroom: palm trees, rustic old forts, and a vast beach. Tybee would be just the thing for a post-exam getaway . . . or at least that's what they thought.

Admitting that she had failed to check the weather before they left campus, Lauren packed for the wretched heat typically felt in July, including shorts, tank tops, and sleeveless shirts. After all, Tybee was on the Atlantic Ocean and not far enough from the Florida border to have a drastic weather difference.

But today, the elements were testing their endurance. Lying face-down on beach towels behind the dunes, the girls were freezing. The sun was in and out of the clouds, and their youthful, shapely bodies were covered in stylish bikinis enhanced by giant goose bumps.

"We should have gone to the Gulf with the rest of the gang," Addy said. "Going back to school without a tan will be so humiliating."

"OK, let's see if we can stand it for another hour," Lauren replied, reaching into the beach bag for another towel to shield herself from the cool breeze. She definitely wasn't thinking straight: The few rays of Tybee sun would have a difficult time penetrating the thick towels covering her.

It was sixty-eight degrees and windy—not exactly prime conditions for spring break. Nonetheless, they chose to stay a little longer and lie sprawled out on top of a pair of sand-filled beach towels, their cold arms tucked beneath their bodies like wings on a bird. Another hour of enduring the cold wind and blowing sand, and they might just leave with a glimmer of a tan. They were two girls on a mission, and it would take more than a fleeting cold front to persuade them to change direction.

Although Tybee Island is an easy drive from town, there are only about 3,500 permanent residents there. This time of the year, the sandy shores and surrounding salt marshes were relatively empty. Occasionally bad things will happen at Tybee. A body might wash up on the beach or be discovered lying under the sand on a dune beneath the walkover.

Addy sat up and, succumbing to the cold, retrieved her sweatshirt. She then surveyed the broad expanse of beach. There was no one in sight for the entire scope of her vision. The surf was getting rougher, and not too far offshore, white-caps were starting to form. Clouds were moving in and it was getting colder, signs they chose to ignore.

Standing up and shaking the sand and blowing debris from their towels, they were startled by something coming out of the surf.

"What is that?" Lauren asked.

"He, or whatever it is, looks strange," Addy replied.

As they watched, engaged in the figure's motion, it seemed to be coming closer and closer to them. It appeared to be a woman coming from the fog billowing off the Atlantic Ocean who was waist deep as she walked up into the shallow water. As they stared and the wind blew even more fiercely, the figure began to slowly stumble toward them. She was covered in a long, period-style dress, and she was drenched. As the surf splashed up against her knees, she traipsed through the foamy surf until she was ankle deep.

"Oh my gosh," said Lauren. "She's coming toward us!"

Crouching down behind the sea oats, the girls panicked. It was too cold to swim, and the woman was too old to fight the rough surf. What was she doing, and why was she there? Neither had to say a word. They both knew that what they were seeing was something surreal.

As soon as her feet touched the dry sand, the woman stopped and began scanning the shoreline. The girls trembled, wondering if she would see them behind the dunes. As they watched speechless, she surveyed the beach. And then she walked toward them in clothes that should have been wet.

"Have you seen my son?" she asked.

"No, ma'am," Addy replied politely, exactly as she had been taught.

The woman then turned and walked away from them silently. She vanished before she reached the water.

Almost simultaneously the girls screamed, "Yikes! What did we just see?"

"We need to leave!" Lauren shouted.

The Frisbee they had brought was blowing down the beach. Lauren raced to retrieve it, but each time she leaned down to pick it up, it would blow farther away. Finally, she gave up as it floated through the air and finally landed on the sand.

And then she saw him. A little boy, about four years old, was sitting to her right, building a castle in the sand.

She ran back to Addy and announced her discovery.

"We're leaving. Now. Quick, find the keys!"

As the girls hastily gathered their belongings and jammed them into their beach bags, they glanced back toward the ocean. Slowly and methodically, they walked away from the child, watching him. They had full intentions of calling the police, but by the time they reached the wooden walkway, he was gone.

Lauren and Addy's spring break was about to be transformed into a personal research project, and the quest for a tan was second only to the mysteries they had discovered on the beach that day. They had witnessed ghosts that had risen out of the surf. The last thing they wanted to do was pretend their day was normal.

The library on Tybee Island was open, and Addy and Lauren raced inside bearing the scent of suntan lotion. They perused the history books and then discovered an article written in 2003 that contained an explanation.

It was 1865 when the SS *Republic,* a side-wheel steamship, began its journey from New York to New Orleans loaded with passengers and freight. The ship had already fulfilled her duties in the Civil War under a different name. Built in Baltimore, Maryland, she was launched in 1853 as the *Tennessee.* Her early years as a merchant ship took her between Baltimore and Charleston, and during the gold rush she transported "gold diggers" to Panama and Nicaragua and to California's Sierra Nevada. As a blockade runner in 1861, the vessel was never able to get through the siege of New Orleans. But following the Union's capture of that city, she soon became a speedy Union weapon in the West Gulf Squadron and a very successful gunship in the Battle of Mobile Bay.

The girls texted their girlfriends while perusing the reference materials, but then came a revelation that demanded their full attention. Laden with more than $500,000 worth of coins, the ship later left New York for New Orleans on a path that would take it directly into the face of a powerful hurricane, just a hundred miles off the coast of Savannah. While many of the passengers survived in four lifeboats, many others died in the forty-foot seas they met that night. The survivors were rescued by the sailing ship *Horace Beals,* while the remainder were lost and perished in the high seas.

Addy and Lauren came upon manifests of those who were pronounced dead, including listings for a mother and small son whose remains were never found. And as far-fetched as it seemed, they agreed that maybe it was these two passengers from that ship that they had met that day on the beach.

Mary Diehl and her son, Robert, were from New Orleans. Sadly, they were on the ill-fated ship, traveling south from New York. They clung to each other until they were sucked under the sea, where they lay for more than a hundred years.

Mother and son, along with the other dead at sea, were in a state of rest . . . that is, until several daring divers sought to explore the wreckage in search of the thousands of gold coins that were on the ship. Because they lacked the equipment and the means to do a thorough search, however, their efforts were stalled.

Finally, in 2003, an expedition to search for the ship's remains, specifically the lost coins, was launched by a company called Odyssey Marine Exploration, Inc., out of Tampa, Florida. And so, armed with sophisticated equipment and a high-tech research vessel, they dove into 1,700 meters of water and began to stir the ocean graves of those who had perished.

Addy and Lauren raced back out to the beach. But when they reached the walkway, they stopped short of the sand.

The clouds were thick with rain, and a storm was moving in from the south. As they stared out onto the beach, they saw the woman, wet and disheveled with ocean debris hanging from her hair. She was searching the beach again.

"There she is!"

Viewing the girls from the beach, the woman walked toward them as they stood breathless.

"I know that you have seen him," she said, her words wafting through the wind.

Lauren pointed down to a shallow gulley near the ocean, directing her toward the sea.

As they watched, the woman met up with the boy and clasped his hand. The girls watched in fear as the pair walked back into the sea until they were swallowed up by the fierceness of the waves. They scampered off the wooden walkway, out onto the street, and into the car, screaming as they ran. With hands trembling, Addy cranked the car and the two turned right off of Sixth Street and onto Butler Avenue, the street that would lead them off the island.

Reaching the curve, Addy hit the break. To the right, lying on its side, was a giant rusted anchor. A stone bearing a weathered description was at its feet. The girls read aloud, almost speaking over each other: ANCHOR, CIRCA 1840. SALVAGED FROM AN OLD WOODEN SAILING SHIP DISCOVERED SEVERAL MILES OFF THE NORTH SHORE OF TYBEE ISLAND.

The sorority house was buzzing with the excitement of the girls being back at college. The dinner bell rang, and Lauren and Addy filed into the dining room with their sisters and sat down for grace. As they started to eat a special back-to-school meal of hamburger steak with mashed potatoes and gravy, the topic they dreaded finally came up.

"So, how was Savannah? Did you do anything fun while you were there?"

It was a snippy sort of question asked by a girl who had recently returned with her family from a Caribbean vacation.

"Well," said Addy, "we saw a ghost on the beach. Actually, we saw two ghosts."

Silence fell over the table, as if somebody had pounded a gavel. They were all looking at Addy.

There was no point in sharing their story. She would forgo the details. She would drop the subject and let them have their talk of Gulf shore flings with preppy college boys and the white sands of south Florida. She and Lauren didn't care. They had fought the chill of spring for a half-roasted suntan and met a pair of spirits who will forever walk the beaches of Tybee Island.

THE FITZROY SAVANNAH

Within an echo of the horns of freighters passing along the riverfront, stands 9 Drayton, an understated building that is said to be the oldest continuously operated saloon and eatery in the historic city. Inside the former home built for Confederate Army officers, the dark brick walls and dimly lit restaurant holds stories and shadows from its past, beginning in 1853 when the building was constructed. Now called The Fitzroy Savannah, little do today's diners realize the story of a brutal murder and evil cover-up that unfolded there years ago still lives inside the brick crevices. Sometimes it's seen in the swaying of a vapor-like body hanging in the back of the main dining room; other times it's heard beneath the restaurant's floors in the painful moans of a man dying. But the terrible story of a good man who died in a drunken brawl still rings true today at the little pub in downtown Savannah.

The charm of an old Savannah pub often lies in its walls that are etched with eerie tales, and The Fitzroy on Drayton has its share of those. Standing three stories high on busy Drayton Street, it's the kind of bar where "everybody knows your name" and diners still relish their last meal there, days after dining there. With rustic brick walls, an original concrete floor with random nicks, and an incredibly peaceful ambiance, it's the kind of place that begs strangers to cozy up for a few hours to solve the world's problems while sipping a cold brew or a Scotch on the rocks.

In the summer, the sign on the door reads COME IN AND COOL OFF. Winter boasts the place's "hot toddies." The rooftop bar is friendly and relaxing, and the chef often emerges from the kitchen and strolls the tables, reassuring the patrons that his dishes are the best in town. The establishment is a place where tourists make return visits and join in friendly conversation with locals who patronize the picturesque bar, some daily.

Built in 1853 by wealthy cotton merchant George W. Anderson, there's nothing fancy about The Fitzroy. The new owners stripped out a massive mahogany bar that infused the room with an old-world style and an elegance. Patrons adored the bar with its splendid alabaster columns and shiny gold fixtures. Many an elbow had rested on that alabaster, and if conversations through the years had been recorded, they would have filled volumes with wise (and foolish) quotations.

But while The Fitzroy projects an image of pleasure and tranquility, it also holds the distinction of being one of Savannah's most frightful and haunted establishments with links to one of the most horrific scandals in the country's history. And through its many years of name changes and owners, some stories are better left untold.

Here's one to be shared.

Former owners and twosome, Gerald and Kristy, were Northerners who ventured to Savannah from Pittsburgh to open the pub that they would name after their grandson, Isaac. They will tell you that apart from their highly acclaimed Southern cuisine and expansive list of beers on tap, during their ownership, there were signs of a terrible ordeal that kept them—and their waitstaff—on edge.

To the average clientele, the couple's menu reflected the establishment's past as a host of boxing matches. The menu was divided into courses of "boxing rounds." Round One offered appetizers from the sea, like grilled shrimp and polenta cake. Round Two focused on the establishment's delicious salads. Round Three, or the main course offerings, included, among other historical reminders, a Beggar's Purse: chicken, collards, and Boursin cheese wrapped in pastry and baked. Isaac's friendly Knock Out Punch, a subtle hint that the pub was once a place where Savannahians gathered for lively sporting events, held a gruesome clue to the building's terrifying past.

The warm and cozy setting of what was then called Isaac's was driven by the building's original owner, a major in the Confederate Army and commander of Fort McAllister in 1864. It was George W. Anderson who happened upon the magnificent bar that brought the pub to life.

Built in the early 1700s in England, it was Anderson who had the former handcrafted bar shipped to New York in several pieces, finally settling in New York's Grand Central Station. While passing through the city in 1853, Anderson found himself sitting on a stool having a drink. As his arm rested on the alabaster railing, he was mesmerized by the intricate details of the dramatic handcrafted piece and decided it would be perfect in his new home and business on Drayton Street. He would live upstairs with his wife, who would decorate the upper floors and operate his establishment on the street level. The bar would become an icon for locals who would come to watch boxing greats in action.

Shipped in pieces from New York in heavy crates, the bar was scrupulously delivered from the ship to Anderson's home on Drayton Street. As the giant crates were pried open, onlookers were shocked by what they found inside.

Curled up in the belly of the rear cabinet was a British stowaway named Bud "Brute" Bailey. Bailey, who had taken temporary work on the New York docks, was overcome by the urge to hide inside the bar that was headed to Savannah. It would be his free ride to a city that held promise for a guy like him.

When the crates were opened and he was exposed, Bailey's body was stiff and weak from the rough voyage south without food or water. Anderson, surprised and impressed by his resilience, invited Bailey to recover in one of the third-floor bedrooms. Little did he realize that his generosity would come at the expense of another and would, to this day, bring fear to those who peer into the windows to this very day.

Bailey regained his strength and began hanging out at the bar inside Anderson's business. His laughter was loud and obnoxious, and the alabaster rail was his object to pound as he shouted at and taunted his nightly companions. Along with his unpleasant behavior, his demeanor soured each day. Soon he became a drunken, boastful man who provoked nearly everyone he met.

One evening while his drunken rampage was just beginning to escalate, a young Savannah Irishman named Jack O'Dwyer sat down beside him. Thin and well-dressed, O'Dwyer was a pillar of professionalism in the community. Bailey, who was brutally drunk, began to poke fun at his new barmate.

"You look like a fool in those glasses, mate," he said boldly. "If I were you, I'd eat a few pounds of beef to rid yourself of those skinny arms."

At first O'Dwyer tried to ignore him, but after a few minutes of Bailey's taunting, he turned to him and said, "Why don't you mind your own business, sir."

"Sir? Did you just call me sir?" Bailey responded, hitting his mug full of beer on the bar so hard that it left a permanent rim. "Why don't you just roll your sleeves up, *sir,* and we'll see who's going to mind the business in this bar!"

O'Dwyer continued to sip his drink, with intentions of leaving, but Bailey was pushing him to an angry response. Then, according to legend, Bailey put forth a challenge to O'Dwyer or anyone else who would brave a bare-knuckle fight.

"Who's going to be brave enough meet my match?" he crowed.

The bar crowd that evening was a mixture of dockworkers, laborers, and a small group of lawyers and businessmen, most of whom backed O'Dwyer.

"I can take him on," O'Dwyer announced to the raucous crowd, throwing down the last ounce of one of his many drinks that night. He wasn't the sort of man to be short-tempered, but after several alcoholic beverages, his boasts became completely out of character.

At first the fight seemed to be nothing more than a friendly slugfest between two drunken men who would soon succumb to exhaustion and quit. But as the minutes turned into the second and then third hour, something went terribly wrong. Bailey's anger escalated into a vicious and cold-blooded state. With one slug after another to O'Dwyer's bleeding head, he continued to beat him with a brutality that Savannahians had never before witnessed.

The crowd watched in horror, hoping someone would step in and call the fight, but it continued with a vengeance. Around 1:00 a.m., O'Dwyer, who had strolled into the bar several hours earlier to have a quick drink before going home, was pronounced dead by one of his friends, who stooped down to the bloodied body and lifted his limp and battered arm off the cold floor of 9 Drayton Street. The crowd rushed over to the man, and a friend called out to the street, begging for the assistance of a doctor, but no one came. Within minutes, three men were seen carrying the bludgeoned body of Jack O'Dwyer down the street to the funeral home a few blocks away.

Appearing to claim a clear victory, Bailey dragged his own body up to the bar. The blood dripping from his arm turned the alabaster rail a light shade of pink.

"I'll have a celebratory whiskey, straight up!" he roared, raising his glass in a toast to himself.

But the crowd had another plan. If they had their way, Bailey would never see the streets of Savannah again.

In the corner of the room, merely feet away from the distinguished mahogany bar, the crowd of onlookers was preparing to publicly torture the man who had murdered a fine Savannah citizen named Jack O'Dwyer. They discreetly prepared a noose for Bailey as he sat at the bar with his back to the crowd. He would soon experience the long-drop method of hanging that breaks the victim's neck by his own weight in a matter of seconds.

As Bailey continued to throw down his drinks, two men approached him, tossing the bloody shirt of O'Dwyer over his head. It took just a few minutes, along with four large men, to string him from the ceiling. As his head bent to the right, snapping his neck like a tree limb, the crowd cheered while the life drained from his dangling body.

The bar's proprietors had plans for Bailey's body. Honorable burials were for honorable men, and because he was a stowaway, there was no record of his citizenship. And because he was so disliked, they began to discuss ways they could dispose of him. They soaked up the blood from the pub's floors, wrapped Bailey's body in thick blankets, and carried him below to the building's cellar, where they dug a deep hole, threw him into it, filled it with dirt, and discreetly returned to their seats at the bar and the normalcy of a rowdy Saturday night.

As the owners from Pittsburgh recalled the events that took place that night, there are still some on the staff of The Fitzroy who are still growing accustomed to the episodes of the past at 9 Drayton. Many evenings they are among those who relive those historical hours. Many nights, patrons report seeing the ghost of Bud "Brute" Bailey and experience strange areas of coldness in the corners of the main dining room. Sometimes Bailey brushes the glasses off the bar, although the place is customarily empty, leaving the day workers to find broken glass shattered across the floor when they arrive the next morning.

No one ever feels alone, they say. There's always a "presence" pushing them along, down the steps, into a patron's table, and even outside into the cold night air or thick, humid heat of summer. When it's closing time, there is a single tea light on the first dining room table that won't go out. And if it does, it will be lit the next morning when the manager opens the restaurant up.

The doors at the rear of the bar never stay closed. Those were the very doors that concealed the stowaway Brute Bailey. Items tend to inexplicably fall inside the walk-in cooler, and some tourists have reported mysterious orbs floating over the bar in photos they have taken while chatting with the bartender.

And on certain nights when people pass by and peer into the windows, they report seeing the image of a bloody body swinging from the rafters toward the back of the room where a boxing ring once stood. More often, they mistake it for a gimmick or restaurant prop. Sometimes they hear the moans of a battered man coming from the dark alley that runs along the side of the building.

There are some things that never change in this age-old establishment, but the turnover rate for bartenders is high. Many claim to be driven out by "something, a presence" that is always casting its breath on their necks while they serve customers.

The bar's owners became fed up with the spirit's annoying efforts to drive them out of the building, so they contacted psychics to study the place. Reports were inconclusive, so they have finally accepted the supernatural presence and tolerate the strange occurrences.

Just a few years ago, the owners had Bailey's body excavated, attempting to rid the place of his spirit. Although his bones were retrieved, his spirit-filled, evil resilience still prevails. If you pass by, you might see him hanging, with his head tied and angling down. Other days, take a seat at the bar and listen for the distinct sound of the bell ringing, signaling another round of horror.

GHOST CAR

The law enforcement manuals did not include a chapter on disappearing cars. That was a subject Officer Greg Jones dodged by choice, even in comedic conversation with his peers. Jones, a three-year veteran of the Garden City Police, was one of the department's most highly regarded officers. On regular patrol one hot Savannah night, he experienced an incident that would prove to be one of the most frightening of his career. It would be an encounter that he would never be able to explain, and one that he would never forget.

There isn't an officer on a police force who would readily admit that he or she enjoys working the night shift, especially in Garden City, Georgia, a small suburb on the west side of Savannah.

The community is like many others, mostly transient, with some homes occupied by retirees and the elderly. Minor fender benders occur during the morning commute, and school zones are a haven for police officers in the market for speedsters. Dotting the smaller residential streets of Garden City are community parks, quaint churches, and a Little League baseball field or two. Mary Caulder Golf Course, located on the outskirts of the International Paper Company's sprawling industrial acreage, is a low-cost draw for avid golfers living nearby. An old-time farmers' market overflowing with fresh vegetables and flowers in the spring and summer makes the community a draw for Savannahians, who drive across the viaduct to buy produce. There's even an eatery serving up homemade vittles anchored to the popular market.

In short and by day, Garden City is a pleasant and desirable place to experience country life near the city of Savannah.

But by night, like many cities today, Garden City is a different story. The small-town atmosphere is replaced by dark streets and lone vagrants who lurk in strip mall parking lots and pass-through industrial thoroughfares with intentions of "being up to no good," according to Southerners. Shoplifting, assault and battery, speeding, driving under the influence, domestic abuse, and robbery are just a few of the crimes listed on a typical day's court docket.

Incorporated in 1939, Garden City is an unusual city with a jurisdiction that links to Interstate 95, a busy pathway for northbound and southbound motorists. As a hub of industry, it's a place that is bustling with several industrial giants, including International Paper. There are a few small parks and some areas dotted with trees, but for the aesthetically conscious, it's not a particularly beautiful town. Viewed from the water, the city's skyline is dotted with the tall cranes of the Georgia Ports Authority and sometimes the silhouettes of the massive container ships docked there. In fact, the Georgia Ports Authority's Garden City location keeps the connecting routes tangled with truck and rail traffic, and during a typical week, accidents are common. The trains constantly pose a risk for drivers crossing the tracks that lead to the shipping terminals, causing daily hazards for police.

The busiest thoroughfare is six lanes wide. Called Augusta Road, it is the home of George A. Mercer Middle School and a steel supply company, along with other small port-related businesses. That road has its share of untidiness, with used car lots on the left and right, pawn shops, a McDonald's, a Dairy Queen, and a few aging strip malls. All are within a stone's throw of traffic and within plain sight of passing cars.

Within the tiny neighborhoods that surround the city's busy roads are modest brick-framed homes occupied by industry workers. There are CHILDREN PLAYING signs cautioning drivers and discouraging speeders. In summary, Garden City is a risky place for high-speed chases.

For Greg Jones, a third-year veteran of the Garden City Police Department, the night shift wasn't all that bad, and he rarely dreaded the dark street patrols. On some nights it could actually be pleasant, while on others the city was a challenging and dangerous place to work, depending on which way the wind was blowing.

Although dealing with risky business was part of the job, on this muggy night when the humidity covered the city like a thick blanket, Greg learned a tough lesson. Even the most astute cops can't fight what they can't catch, especially if the driver is a ghostly vapor and the vehicle mysteriously vanishes without explanation.

Donning his bulletproof vest, pressed uniform, peripheral gear, and gleaming weapon, Greg washed down a quick sandwich with a Coke and headed out the door for his twelve-hour shift, hoping for an easy and uneventful night. He would be off for the following two days and planned to catch up on yard work after his usual five hours of sleep.

He started his patrol in one of the city's smaller neighborhoods, cruising down a side street and tipping his hat to a family sitting on their porch, enjoying the sultry night. Turning onto busy Augusta Road, he never realized that the calm of this night was about to turn into a terrifying escapade.

His shift was nearing the halfway mark when he pulled into a convenience store around 11:30 p.m. for a cup of coffee. While he sat in his patrol car, sipping coffee and surveying the few passing cars, an older model white car sped past him, heading west on Augusta Avenue toward the link to busy I-95 high-traffic interstate. As quickly as it had passed him, the call came over the radio: An older model white sedan—tag unknown—was traveling at excessive speeds and had almost hit a pedestrian crossing the road. It was that call that would convince Greg of the elusive powers of the supernatural.

Tossing the coffee as if it were burning his hands, he gathered his wits, turned on his flashing blue lights, and hit the accelerator, being careful not to endanger the few cars that were on the road. As standard in most police vehicles, he checked to make sure his camera was set to record the action.

As his squad car climbed to speeds well over ninety miles per hour, he suddenly realized that he would never catch up with the sedan as he controllably sped along. By now Greg was sweating. In constant radio contact with his department, he had asked for backup from the state highway patrol and Savannah Police Department. But as he tried to keep up, it appeared that he would be the lone officer in pursuit. Accelerating to the very brink his car could tolerate, he could not catch up to the sedan, which was swerving across both lanes at high speeds, leaving him lagging behind. In, out, across the road, left, right it sped, possessed by an unknown driver. Greg's calmness was turning to anger, and his patience was waning.

Suddenly the sedan stopped, and in an instant, started heading in the opposite direction. When Greg turned around, he caught a glimpse of the driver's vapor-like head, which slumped in the seat like a dummy with no neck. Man? Woman? He couldn't tell. But what he could tell was that whatever it was, it did not have a "solid" head. The speeding car was headed toward the interstate exit, and Greg's challenge was to keep it away from other motorists. If he didn't stop the car, there could be accidents with injuries, or even fatalities, on the traffic-laden interstate.

"He's about to pull over," Greg said to dispatch.

Then, without a hint, the car suddenly vanished.

"He's gone. I don't see him anywhere," Greg radioed.

All of a sudden, the sedan appeared in front of him out of nowhere, once again swerving back and forth across the road as if the vehicle itself were possessed, reaching speeds that Greg's patrol car was not capable of handling. Then suddenly, as it sped along on the straightaway, it turned sharply left and directly into a chain-link fence barrier along the highway. Greg slammed on his brakes, barely missing the fence, and watched in shock as the sedan's taillights went completely out of his view.

Dust blew up onto his patrol car's camera lens.

"He's gone," Greg said. "My God, he just plowed through the chain-link fence."

Stepping out of his car, he stared at the fence, which was untouched. He then walked alongside it, feeling the strength of the thick wire, wondering how it could be.

There have been reports all over the world about cars that mysteriously appear and then vanish. In Germany, a car reportedly started up and drove away without a driver. In the 1960s, a northeastern U.S. newspaper reported that a car had passed another vehicle, and then kept reappearing behind the vehicle it had just passed. This type of "phantom vehicle" can be one that appears seemingly out of nowhere, racing at high speeds, and then suddenly and without explanation disappears.

While training at the police academy at nearby Georgia Southern University, Greg and his buddies had joked about Savannah's reputation as "the most haunted city in America." Although he hadn't personally had any ghostly encounters during his early career in law enforcement, Greg had been warned that there were "spirits" in and around the city that posed potential mental threats to otherwise healthy and astute officers. Greg couldn't have dreamed that he would—on an unusually normal night—be in hot pursuit of an elusive force.

As he drove back to the station in disbelief, Greg could hardly wait to review his camera's videotape. His mind ventured back to his younger days and *The Twilight Zone*—it was just like the old black-and-white TV show he had been obsessed with as a child. But this was a mystery he couldn't solve on his own. An intact fence, straight up, with no gaps, had provided the speedster with an escape that his camera recorded. The vapor-like driver plowed right through it and completely vanished without even touching the barrier.

There are legitimate definitions of the term "phantom vehicle." In the insurance industry, "a phantom vehicle causes bodily injury, death, or property damage to an uninsured vehicle." In this case, there is no physical contact. And then there's the definition that is common to those who have seen, but cannot explain, a vehicle that mysteriously appears with or without a driver. That was the definition fresh on the mind of the young police officer that hot night in Georgia.

Print media coverage of the episode went nationwide. Greg Jones's name as one who had "chased a ghost car" was all over the media. After a few weeks, he received a call from a show called *Fact or Faked: Paranormal Files* on the Syfy channel. The tape of the phantom car chase has been shown time after time, with no logical explanation.

The Garden City Police are on constant watch for the phantom car. Meanwhile, Greg has moved on to another department in another town, often returning to the video posted on YouTube, to study the recording of his night spent chasing an elusive spirit.

BURIED ALIVE

What started as a leisurely carriage ride through Savannah's Historic District ended after midnight in one of the city's most haunted burial grounds, Colonial Park Cemetery. For one family in town for a vacation, the tour that they imagined would be slightly entertaining would become a lesson in horror.

The family of four from Oregon had been waiting for twenty minutes to climb aboard a carriage tour scheduled to pick them up in the center of Savannah's City Market. It was going on 10:00 p.m., and by all standards, it was getting to be almost too late to view the streets of the Historic District. But they had listened intently to the clip-clop of horses' hooves going by as they dined outside on the veranda of an eatery, and the serenity of a horse-drawn carriage was just what they needed on this, their third day in Savannah. It would be the perfect diversion for the kids, who were bored after a day spent on foot reading monuments. Plus, there would be a certain edge to touring Savannah by carriage to the tune of spooky tales.

They had bypassed the standard tours billed as "popular" and opted for one less publicized, hoping for some authenticity. Booking online, they never spoke to anyone from the company, but trust and a quick online credit card payment prompted a hasty email confirmation. Billed as a two-hour ride through the city's Historic District, they were instructed to bring a jacket and bottled water, and to make sure they had transportation back to their hotel once the tour had ended. What the online instructions failed to say was where the tour would end.

They had read in a recently published guidebook that the personality of the tour guide is often the key to a successful tour, and if the book was accurate, this tour would certainly make up for the tardiness of the driver. Besides, it was their summer vacation, and it really didn't matter what time the tour ended. So as the band blared from the City Market courtyard, they waited as 10:00 p.m. turned to 10:15.

Shortly after 10:15, the carriage pulled up, and an older woman wearing a ruffled blouse and stylish black hat ushered them aboard. She never introduced herself, and with her back toward her guests, she held the reins, directed them to get comfortable, and mumbled something under her breath. Savannah's spookiest tales were about to unfold, or so they thought.

"There's something strange about her," ten-year-old Todd whispered to his sister, Sarah. "She's weird, and I don't like it." Blair, the father, scolded the children, "Quiet! Don't be rude."

Winding through Johnson Square in silence, they felt the giant live oaks looked all the more frightful at night. Their thick branches were overgrown and covered with moss, casting a tentlike cover over the fountains, monuments, and park benches. The scene resembled a the set of *A Nightmare on Elm Street*, minus the popcorn. As the clip-clop of the old mare passed a street vendor who was packing up for the night, the guide looked up at the massive columns of Christ Church as if she were about to say something about the structure. Then she looked down toward the sidewalk and began speaking to someone, but there was no one in sight.

The backseat whispers were at an all-time high.

"So far, this tour and the driver are the only creepy things we've seen," said Todd. "But I do like the horse."

They had already passed one of Savannah's most splendid landmarks, Christ Church, and there was not a mention of the building's history, let alone its spirits. The family at least had the guidebook as a reference as they continued around the circle and southward. "There's a bell inside that church," Todd said. "It was made by the Revere and Sons. Hey, weren't they famous or something? Oh, whatever."

The driver was silent as she steered the carriage southward without stopping or saying a word. As they crossed Broughton Street, she waved to passing motorists, although there was no traffic on the street.

Where was she taking them, and why wasn't she sharing the tales that made Savannah famous? They were beginning to feel unnerved, and the family who had signed up for the ghost tour by carriage was becoming all the more disturbed by the driver's silence.

Soon they stopped in front of the magnificent John S. Norris—designed Mercer House, built in 1869 and named for General Hugh Mercer. Mercer was the grandfather of the famous Savannah songwriter Johnny Mercer. The home was purchased by Jim Williams, the famous preservationist and the subject of John Berendt's book *Midnight in the Garden of Good and Evil* a few years back. As the family gazed upon the house that was framed by hearty palm trees, the driver waved again.

"Hello, Jim," she said. "That's Jim Williams standing there on the sidewalk. He's the owner of the house."

Bristling in her seat, Ann, the mother, grasped the arm of her husband, Blair. She knew for certain that Jim Williams was deceased. She had both read and watched the *Midnight* story, and that very afternoon the family had toured the home with a guide who claimed, "There are no ghosts in Mercer House. This is a house full of joy."

Whispering in her husband's ear, Ann said, "I'm sure we've gotten on the wrong tour. This woman is strange."

"Hope you enjoyed Monterey Square," the driver said. "Now it's on to my favorite part of the tour."

No ghosts? Little history? It was going on midnight, and yawns were coming from the children, who by this time had snuggled beneath a blanket. With safety in mind, Ann looked at her watch. This was not the time to be touring Savannah. Yet, as the sound of the horse's hooves kept a steady rhythm that was almost mesmerizing, it appeared as though they were going farther and farther south from their start in City Market.

As they reached Oglethorpe by way of Drayton, they turned left, and in a few minutes, stopped in front of Colonial Park Cemetery. The guide, who had her back turned to the family, stepped off the carriage and ordered them to follow her to the gate. Normally opened during the day and closed at dark, the gate was propped just wide enough to fit through.

With a flashlight in hand, Todd began reading from the guidebook.

"This cemetery was originally the burial ground for the members of Christ Church. It was established in 1750 on about six acres of land, and in 1789 it was opened to people of all denominations."

The driver asked the family to follow her through the dark and desolate grounds, and while they attempted to navigate the terrain, they found themselves tripping over gravestones.

"It says here that there are ghosts in the cemetery," Todd said, continuing to read from the guidebook. "It says there's a famous ghost here named Rene something, who was accused to murdering two girls right here in this area."

"Stop, you're scaring me," Sarah said, clinging to her mother's pant leg.

The driver continued walking past the gravestones and finally stopped near a long brick wall that appeared studded with stone markers.

"That looks very creepy. Let's get out of here," Ann whispered to the others. She grabbed their hands, and they began backing away slowly.

By day it would have been easy to see that this was the east wall of the cemetery, with markers that were worn from the years. Nearby the graves of James Habersham, Button Gwinnett, General Samuel Elbert, and Archibald Bulloch stood.

Passing the wall, the driver made a startling statement.

"See that grave? Well, that's mine."

She then turned toward the family, and they witnessed a terrible sight as they slowly retreated. In place of her eyes were deep holes covered in a hazy white glare. There were no pupils, just solid white circles. And when she spoke, blood seeped from the corners of her mouth. They froze.

No wonder she wouldn't turn around before. No wonder she hadn't introduced herself.

Frozen and fearful of her next move, the family stood like soldiers in the darkened graveyard, afraid to say anything or move for fear that she might seize them.

"I was buried alive," she continued. "There was a sickness going around that the doctors called yellow fever. First, my sister contracted it. She died. Then I became very ill, and on the night when the doctor came and told my parents that I was dead, I was placed in a coffin and buried here.

"But I wasn't really dead. I scratched the lid of the coffin with all my might, trying to make my escape. But I was too weak to pry open the top. As I lay there in misery, I could hear the occasional sounds of bells ringing. Those were the sounds of victims who had been buried with their hands tied to bells that hung out from the casket. There were so many people buried alive here, they did that so a live person in a casket could ring a bell for help. It was a way to get the attention of those who were taking care of the burial grounds. They were aware that some of victims of the disease put into graves were not really dead. When I appeared to stop breathing, they declared me dead and put me away without a rope, much less a bell.

"I eventually died. I really don't know how long it took once they put me underground. Oh, and I went with my parents to Christ Church. I recall reciting the Lord's Prayer, kneeling on the bench, saying the words, 'Our father, who art in heaven . . .' I never made it to heaven. But I'm here to torment those who have made a business out of our fate. People like you come and pay to laugh and joke and see where it all happened."

Todd led the way, followed by Sarah and their parents. They ran in unison, often jumping the gravestones and at times stumbling, and finally made their way onto Abercorn Street and the corner where the headquarters of the Savannah Fire Department stood like a mirage in a desert. They pounded on the door and were met by a smiling face who invited them in, calmed them and kindly called a cab. It was 1:00 a.m., and the family from Oregon had finally completed their ghost tour.

As they stood on the street corner waiting for the cab to arrive, they heard a familiar sound in the distance.

Clip, clop, clip, clop.

Maybe the misfortune of this carriage tour driver would never end. Perhaps she would drive the carriage through the streets of Savannah forever, fearful of returning to the coffin again. If you listen closely, you can sometimes hear the sounds of her horse as she spills her grief over the cobblestone streets of Savannah's downtown. And if you're brave enough to buy a ticket on a carriage tour, be sure to stare into the face of the driver before you board.

HAUNTINGS FROM THE HOSPITAL

For years the old Candler Hospital has been the object of Savannahians' love and affection. From retired physicians and nurses who started their careers at Candler to elderly adults who were born there, the venerable structure is an iconic tribute to life in this Southern city. Today, it has new life as it was purchased by the Savannah College of Art and Design and redesigned. It holds its place as a stunning renovation and is now known as Ruskin Hall. But rarely told are the tales of the building's dark side, and years of dormancy that have left time and space for spirits to dwell, often keeping developers away. Will there be someone walking the new halls at the art school who is touched by a spirit still dwelling there? Only time will tell.

The weathered black-and-white real estate sign in front of the old Warren A. Candler Hospital contained a simple message: OFFICE SPACE AVAILABLE. Prominently situated off a busy street in the Historic District, it was one of those places that people occasionally talked about when there was a lull in the conversation.

"I wonder why somebody doesn't do something with the old Candler building," they said.

While the sign provided a modern-day contrast to the aging property, there were few parties interested in immediate occupancy. The building sat dormant, month after month, through the humid haze of Savannah's steamy summers and the occasional frosts of her winter. In some places the architectural elements were stunning, even while the elements beat down heat and fed the interior mold.

It was probably the sign that attracted the Columbia, South Carolina, real estate developer to inquire about the stately old building. Although it had seen its share of short-term tenants, he was aware of the building's availability and could somehow foresee the promises of revitalization.

Commercial real estate developer Nathan Cogwell dialed the number without reservation. He had ordered a scout from his office to seek out some prospective buildings for renovation in Savannah. When his scout returned with news of a potential project, Cogwell followed his instincts and called to inquire.

A sweet voice on the other end of the line politely scheduled a lunch meeting with Cogwell and his two-man team—a contractor and an architect. Afterward, they would spend several hours touring the structure that boasted a captivating lesson in history, including some eerie chapters.

The evolution of the well-built complex had taken it from a hospital for the poor, to a Civil War medical facility, to a medical college, and finally to its most prestigious use as a well-known and highly respected hospital. It was 1931 when the Methodist-owned facility was christened the Warren A. Candler Hospital, in honor of a bishop. Since the facility closed in 1980 to relocate to midtown Savannah, the old site had garnered little attention and few rental clients. It begged for a developer's touch.

Cogwell was enthusiastic about the site's potential. He would arrive armed with visions of transforming the two-building project into rental studio apartments for art college students. His plans called for small apartments that would be supported by ground-level retail shops, a restaurant, and office space. His previous projects in Savannah were deemed highly successful, and his ability to take dilapidated structures and turn them into useful and value-growing real estate had already been demonstrated, winning the approval of locals and, more importantly, Savannah's Historic Review Board.

Savannah broker Brooks Murphy was equally excited. The building had been a crumbling eyesore for several years, and with each year that it sat untouched, it would require more money and time to renovate all of its expansive 110,000 square feet of space. Murphy rarely received inquiries about the building, which was constructed in 1808, as its exterior, although functionally sound, was beginning to show its age.

The 2010 economic decline had produced a dramatic drop in commercial real estate prospects, and Cogwell's call was very much welcomed by Murphy, who spent his days struggling to market his properties as the economy turned downward. Murphy was aware that there was a dark side to the aging structure that was rarely discussed. Would this prospective developer from Columbia focus on its exceptionally outstanding pre–Civil War construction, or would he and his team leave spooked, like the rest of his prospective clients?

Murphy had read the article by William H. Whitten that appeared in the *Savannah Morning News* in the 1950s about "secret autopsies" that were practiced in the basement and hidden passageways beneath the hospital. In the article, Whitten quoted a noted Savannahian who recalled playing in the tunnel as a child while her grandfather, a physician, scolded her for getting too close to a place infested with germs that carried diseases. It is said that a physician and two members of his staff died from their work trying to diagnose a disease called yellow fever that was killing Savannahians. It was also reported that the spirits of those who had died in the basement still occupied the space below. Although Murphy had never seen signs of this, he was cautious whenever he showed the property.

There were other terrible stories about the old Candler Hospital, and Murphy hoped to avoid sharing the dreadful history of the building with his new client. He was determined to keep his words professional and minimal.

For years, ghost tour operators teased tourists with promises of taking them inside the building and underground through the "spooky tunnels." But liability issues interfered, and the Savannah Metro Police Department frowned on such visits. They constantly patrolled the area, running off vagrants, curiosity seekers, and occasionally small groups of goth college students.

How could Murphy focus on sharing the positive aspects of the hospital's past while hiding the secrets and chilling reminders of war, death, destruction, and yes, even spirits? He would attempt to charm his clients with a grand performance as a true Southern gentleman, while remaining tight-lipped regarding the terrible stories he had heard of the property's history.

Called the Savannah Poor House and Hospital Society when it opened in 1808, the facility later became a central location for treating wounded soldiers during the War between the States. Death and suffering defined its role, and there was little joy coming from the place. Outside, a grand live oak still stands majestically in the parking area. To this day, that icon is represented in the new hospital's logo.

To historians, the structure represents a stately landmark and a reminder of all the roles the building played in nurturing the city's historic past. After Sherman occupied Savannah, it was transformed into a Union hospital before becoming a medical college and undergoing renovation in 1876.

In the summers of the 1800s, yellow fever, a disease that was thought to be contagious at first, spread through Savannah. Between several epidemics, nearly 4,000 people lost their lives to the disease. Carried by mosquitoes, yellow fever was indeed deadly. As the epidemic spread, Candler's halls became both morgues and recovery areas as rooms were filled to capacity with gravely ill patients.

There were severe shortages of physicians and nurses, in addition to space to house the ill patients. It is said that the hallways were filled with rolling beds bearing patients, both living and dead, lying side by side. Also reported in the archives of Savannah's history are the cries of misery of those who lost children or parents, often as they lay in the same bed, dying.

Crying children were often seen running through the hospital in search of their parents who had passed away, and at times, newly born babies were suffocated by their own mothers to spare them from the living hell that was tormenting the people of Savannah.

During the epidemic a sloping tunnel was connected to the basement, and pine boxes bearing the dead were rolled down the chilled ramp-like enclosure below Drayton Street and into the darkness of the night. Across the street was a spread of woods where they were secretly buried—some by mistake, still alive within their simple caskets. Today, people in cars pass over the closed tunnel without the knowledge that below them was once a narrow, dark morgue.

Reports from a few locals who have entered the tunnel reveal that a stone table and basin still stand, signs that the victims may have undergone experimental autopsies. Furthermore, their body parts—heads, limbs, and torsos—were disposed of discreetly and haphazardly. Skulls, arms, and legs were sometimes found in the most surprising places.

These accounts of the building's history weren't exactly script-worthy for a real estate broker's sales pitch or glamerous brochures with enticing photos.

Cogwell's team arrived in Savannah at noon on a beautiful spring day when the city was blazing with color. The azaleas were in full bloom, and all around were signs of this Southern city's annual rebirth. After lunch, Cogwell's group and Murphy proceeded to the hospital in separate cars and parked in the rear of the building near the grand oak tree. Admiring its beauty, they walked around to the Habersham Street side, where the chains on the doors were unlocked. As they entered what was once the hospital's waiting area, a sudden cold burst of air engulfed the room, and within a minute, they found themselves pale, shivering, and achy, as though they had the flu.

"The air-conditioning doesn't work, of course, but it's chilly in here. This is a really old building, you know," said Murphy, trying to create optimism in his sales presentation.

"Wow," said Cogwell, as he stepped into the cold and gloomy foyer. "We could gut the floors above and create a wonderful atrium that would brighten the entranceway and be architecturally outstanding." The contractor placed his tool-box down on the floor and retrieved a measuring tape, recording the dimensions and sketching the existing wall positions in a small notebook. As he placed the tape measure back into the box, he noticed that his level was missing. And when he glanced back at his notebook, his notes and sketches were covered with scribble. His hands were icy and his body was overcome with joint pain so severe, he couldn't comprehend the mysterious happenings that were occurring right before his very eyes.

Murphy's cell phone rang, and he asked to be excused.

"Here's a simple layout of the building. I'll step outside, take this call, and catch up with you in a bit," he said, pleased to have an excuse to get out.

The scent of stale antiseptic mixed with the odor of fresh blood was overwhelming as the three gentlemen slowly walked down the hallway, peering into the small rooms that once had been occupied by patients. They proceeded cautiously, with a sense of dread rather than curiosity. Suddenly, an outdated fluorescent fixture that had been dangling above them fell from the ceiling and crashed to the ground, just after they passed beneath it. It sounded like a gunshot through glass.

"Wow, we should have worn hard hats," Cogwell said in a gruff voice, touching his head only to realize that he *was* wearing a hard hat.

The contractor, armed with a camera, began snapping pictures while they stood in disbelief, still shocked by the deafeningly loud crash.

"It was probably caused by the building settling," he said, trying to reserve his true hypothesis and shivering uncontrollably from the cold.

As they turned the corner of the long hallway, they stopped abruptly. The sound of a woman crying "Help me!" could be heard loud and clear. The cries became fainter as they continued; however, no one dared to bring it up. Each of the three thought that they might be hallucinating or coming down with something as they toured the vacant building.

The contractor's camera continued to capture the grim images of empty operating rooms and recovery areas, and as he snapped, the building became colder and colder. The conversation soon switched to leaving and "beating the traffic."

The contractor no sooner said, "We'd better get back on the road soon," when they were overwhelmed by the strong scent of spoiled institutional-type food. As it became even stronger, they were overcome with nausea. Using their sleeves to ward off the scent, they continued down the stairs to the basement as if they were being magically pulled there.

Out of nowhere, Murphy's cheery voice broke the silence and startled the threesome as they came to the bottom of the stairwell.

"Where've y'all been?"

Murphy was becoming an annoyance, and his cheerful sales pitch was having the opposite effect, turning the group away from the plans for restoration.

Hoping that Cogwell wouldn't ask about the basement and what had transpired there, Murphy took a deep breath. He turned on his cheery sales pitch voice in an attempt to divert the subject.

"There's about five thousand square feet of basement that would be perfect as storage."

And then the dreaded question popped up.

"So, uh, what did this used to be?" Cogwell asked as he blew a puff of warm air into his cold hands.

The digital camera that the contractor was using was beginning to fog up in the damp basement, but he continued to take shots of the area.

Murphy, exhausted and freezing, suddenly blurted out the truth.

"Medical experiments were conducted here in this basement when the Savannah Medical College took it over from 1871 to 1888. We think there were autopsies performed here for educational purposes. They cut off the heads of some subjects, and a few years ago an old barrel was recovered with grotesque remains—the subjects' skulls."

What on earth had made him speak those words? If only he could take them back.

As the men tried to ignore Murphy's answers, which were getting more morbid by the minute, the contractor felt a strong urge to go deeper into the area, as if something were pushing him in the direction of a massive metal door. With camera in hand, he walked over to the door. Pushing it open, he peered down into a hole about six feet tall and barely over four feet wide.

"What's this?" he asked.

"Uh, that's where the bodies of those who died from disease were transported out of the hospital," Murphy replied.

To the right a few feet down, the men forced themselves to look. Floating in the shallow, filthy water that was laden with the debris from vagrants, was a human bone—possibly a femur. While one end was rounded to match up with its socket, the other end was sawed off, a practice performed during the Civil War by physicians amputating limbs.

"Is there anything else you should tell me about this place?" Cogwell asked Murphy sternly.

The men then headed up the stairs and hurried down the hall and out the front door, into the air warmed by the afternoon sun.

As they continued their conversation outside, the contractor popped his camera's card into his laptop resting on the trunk of the car. The final image that he had shot of the eerie basement on the way out was enlarged and clear on his screen. Shielding the screen from the sun, he stared at the image and gasped.

Within the frame, scrawled in a blood-like red substance, were the letters LEAVE.

"As a matter of fact, there is one thing I failed to tell you," Murphy was saying. "The old Candler Hospital building has been said to be the most haunted structure in America."

Cogwell and his team hastily got into their car, nearly colliding to get in. Cogwell bid Murphy good-bye, thanking him sarcastically for his "tour of a building we hope never to enter again."

Today, the OFFICE SPACE AVAILABLE sign is gone. The Savannah Law School faded away; after only a few years occupying and renovating the space, it closed. If you drive past the site, you'll see a lovely building in the traditional Savannah exterior style with a contemporary and modern interior. Art school students are in and out the door, working creatively to boost their post-college careers. The sign out front says Ruskin Hall, but if you glance out your window, be forewarned: Signs can be deceiving. The events of the past still live within the walls and under the building. Wait until the doors are locked and stand outside. You'll hear the cries of those spirits who still live in the old Candler Hospital.

HABERSHAM HALL

When an animation student from China arrived in Savannah, he never dreamed that his English classroom in beautiful Habersham Hall would prove to be more than a place to study. One evening when he reported there for tutoring, he learned a little more than the basics of the English language. What he saw would make him wish he had chosen a different class in a different building.

As a freshman at the Savannah College of Art and Design (SCAD), Ming was doing well and growing accustomed to life in the United States. Originally from Hong Kong, he had traveled to Savannah to study animation, a program (one of many) that had put SCAD on the map. Ming enjoyed his walks through the beautiful Historic District, where his classes were easily accessible by foot. Although his living quarters in the dorm were tiny, they were convenient to everything he needed: classrooms, grocery stores, and school facilities. He could walk most anyplace he needed to go and, therefore, live car-free. All was going well for Ming with his new life in the South, except for one major obstacle: His English was terrible.

A transition team was provided by the college to assist the school's international student community. The first thing they recommended was for Ming to sign up for "English as a Second Language," one of the most popular classes among SCAD's foreign students.

Taught by Elizabeth Turner, a petite woman from Pittsburgh who could pass for a student herself, the class proved to be difficult for Ming. He struggled with all aspects of the language—spelling, grammar, and speech—but looked forward to attending the class on Mondays and Wednesdays. He was amazed by the beauty of Habersham Hall, a castle-like building that resembled the magical structures in Hong Kong, on a street filled with otherwise stodgy buildings.

His instructor was sympathetic to his difficulties and eager to help, but even after making English his priority, Ming continued to struggle. Miss Turner suggested tutoring at 7:00 p.m. on Tuesdays, and he gladly accepted her offer. They would meet in Room 210, with its tall ceiling and beautiful wood floor. Ming was grateful for Miss Turner's kindness, and she reminded him of his mother, who was also tiny in stature. She also wore a pleasing fragrance reminiscent of the sweet-smelling roses in his favorite flower shop, Beloved Home, in Hong Kong. So, with optimism, Ming happily committed to weekly tutoring.

Habersham Hall is one of Savannah's most striking and unusual buildings. While most buildings are characteristic of a specific style and period, this one is an example of "Moorish Revival." The three-story structure was built in 1887 and designed by the McDonald brothers (Harry and Kenneth) of Louisville, Kentucky. Unlike so many other buildings in Savannah's downtown, however, it was not constructed as a home for a wealthy cotton merchant, but rather to house the worst of criminals.

According to records in the SCAD library, a residence was built at one end for a jailer, and a long cellblock that ran the length of Habersham Street encompassed the remainder. Plans called for 117 cells, two basement dungeons, a cell for condemned prisoners, an infirmary, and a ninety-three-foot-high clock tower. Male and female prisoners would be separated.

The completed building was more than forty thousand square feet and constructed with extra-thick granite flooring in the jailer's residence and the cells. City planners heralded the design when it was completed and marveled at its trademark onion dome. After a fire in 1898 damaged the Byzantine-style dome, a striking Moorish turret replaced it. Towering above the street at 106 feet, the turret's accents consisted of four cast-iron balconies that were used until 1978.

The property was donated to the college in 1986 and completely renovated to the acclaim of faculty and students. What was once an old county jail was now a stunning classroom facility for art school students from all over the world, and Ming was grateful for the opportunity to experience the college's renovation project firsthand.

Ming's first Tuesday-evening tutoring session was about thirty minutes away from starting. Stopping first by Gallery Expresso downtown for a chai latte, he headed for Habersham Hall with his backpack slung over his shoulder. Balancing his books and the drink while walking on the uneven sidewalks of downtown was a challenge, but he was cautious, trying to sip his tea and still get there on time.

As Ming neared the iron-gated building, he paused to look upward. Habersham Hall was a bit disturbing at dusk, almost like a contrived movie set or the haunted mansion he had seen at Disney World. All of the windows were gated with the crossed, sturdy bars that once kept prisoners from escaping. The iconic iron balconies on the towering turret looked as though they were built for guards to stand on and overlook the grounds. As he walked up to the front of the building, he could see lights on in Room 210. When he entered the room, Miss Turner was waiting with her smile and sweet-smelling fragrance. Ming was also relieved to see two other students from China.

The tutoring session went well, and Ming seemed to be catching on. Miss Turner gave him several study sheets to complete prior to class the next morning. He could tell this was going to be a long night.

The first to leave, he packed up and scurried down the stairs and onto the sidewalk. And then he stopped.

A dreadful sound was coming from the tower. It was almost as if the innards of a passing car were dragging on the street. Ming looked around to see if there was any traffic that could be causing such a ruckus. He saw nothing, but just as he started to resume walking, the sound again rang out from the building—this time, louder than before.

Ming turned around and ran back inside, into the room where Miss Turner and the other students were still working. In broken English, he struggled to relate his fears.

"What can, uh, afraid, I am, loud sound," he said. Miss Turner and the students acknowledged the commotion, but, continued to forge on through the lessons.

Ming turned and ran out of the building, thankful that his return the next morning would be during daylight hours. But the next morning when he arrived for his 10:00 a.m. class, the sound returned as he walked closer to the building.

Ming tried to ignore it and attempted to hypothesize. Maybe there was construction going on around the corner in the rear of the building? Or maybe there was a mechanical problem with the heating system? But although he was nervously alert for "the sound," during class time he never shared his concerns with the other students.

The weekend came, and Ming decided to chance a stroll by Habersham Hall at dusk.

As soon as he passed the front gate, the grinding started. Ming raced to the local convenience store and deli around the corner. He needed to be around other people, and although he opted to remain silent, he decided to stay clear of Habersham Hall as much as possible.

It was 1888, the year after Habersham Hall was constructed. The building was nearing its limit, with prisoners packed into the cells. There was one small dungeon room that was empty; however, it bore a reservation for its next occupant.

It had taken a couple of days to travel the mostly dirt roads by automobile from Charleston to Savannah. Charles, a wealthy banker from the North, was bringing his new bride, Jane, to Savannah for their wedding trip. The journey was exhausting, and their driver had become ill around Beaufort. Charles took the wheel as Jane sat by his side and the driver slept in the rear.

Darkness was setting in as they rode over the narrow wooden bridge across the salt marshes near Savannah. The couple fought sleep, sometimes dozing off for a few seconds, as the last leg of the journey wore on. Visibility was poor, and Charles had difficulty keeping the horseless carriage in line with the road. All of a sudden, they hit something. The hard thump alerted his bride, and the driver let out a low moan.

"What was that?" Charles asked, trying to keep control of wheel.

Climbing out vehicle, he reached down to find a man lying there, maimed or dead from the hit. Charles was not just taken aback, he was horrified!

Charles felt for a pulse and then declared the man dead. His bride began to weep.

"We are murderers. We will surely be hanged or imprisoned for killing this man," Jane sobbed.

But Charles, a man wise from many business successes, devised a plan.

"We will report the death of this man," he said. "But we will blame the accident on our driver."

When they reached Savannah, they turned the body of the man struck and killed by Charles over to the police, along with his "killer." As the ill driver was taken away in shackles to the jail and placed in the dungeon below, he cursed the couple. "I will live to declare that I was not responsible for this man's death."

Charles and Jane enjoyed their stay in Savannah's finest hotel and danced until dawn their first night in town. Silly from champagne and comfortable that no one would suspect that Charles was driving the night of the accident, they spent their days in Savannah dining and socializing with the city's elite. Meanwhile, imprisoned in Habersham Hall, their driver remained shackled in the dungeon of the city's jail for a crime he didn't commit.

The weekend flew by, and Ming was beginning to speak and understand the English language well. Miss Turner commended him after class on Monday morning, and he was becoming more confident of his newly learned skills. Tutoring classes were paying off, and the upcoming Tuesday-evening session would more than likely be his last.

The following day, as he entered the building and ran up the stairs to the second floor, he heard "the sound." This time, it was accompanied by the faint figure of a man in shackles. Room 210 was dark and no one was inside, including Miss Turner.

Ming called out to the figure that he could now only barely hear chanting a word that he did not recognize. Running out the door, he looked up onto the balcony of the turret. But, as always, the balcony was empty.

He couldn't sleep that night, so he searched the Internet for the word spoken by the spirit he had seen. There were two definitions. The first read: "Innocent: not guilty of a specific crime or offense; legally blameless." Ming was satisfied that the figure he had heard and seen in Habersham Hall was a tormented soul trapped within that building. Ironically, the second definition of the word hit close to his heart: "Innocent: not exposed to or familiar with something specified."

Ming realized that upon his arrival in America, he was "innocently" deprived of the English language.

Innocent. Yes. He understood the definition of that word.

The next morning, he couldn't wait to tell Miss Turner about the ghost he had seen, but it was a little early for class. Strolling over to the cemetery directly across the street, Ming followed his instincts to a headstone lying in an area with no other graves nearby. He would no longer have to struggle reading the words. His new language skills were definitely at work.

As he gazed down at the headstone, he once again heard the disturbing sound, only this time, it was louder. This time it was coming from Habersham Hall's turret. He looked up to see the same vision he had witnessed the night before. Diverted by the sound but intent on reading the stone, he slowly spoke the words aloud: HERE LIE THE REMAINS OF JONATHAN CAM, DISTINGUISHED BUTLER FROM CHARLESTON, SOUTH CAROLINA. HE FOUGHT FOR HIS INNOCENCE TO NO AVAIL.

Miss Turner would likely be impressed.

As for Jonathan Cam, Ming had already accepted his plea. He would no longer fear the chains he heard each time he entered and left Habersham Hall.

He understood. Peace would never come to the driver who would serve his time after death in eternal shackles.

THE SPIRITS OF THE SHRIMP FACTORY

The evolution of an old cotton warehouse embraces tragedies that are centuries apart. Yet even those closest to the space that now attracts tourists by the hundreds can't figure out who abides in the storage room upstairs at the Shrimp Factory. Could it be the spirit of an old, loyal warehouse employee, or an employee who suffered a massive heart attack unexpectedly in the 1970s? The debate among the current employees is ongoing.

An advertisement placed prominently inside the April 29, 1848, issue of *The Georgian,* a state newspaper, was enticing to wealthy cotton merchants seeking space along Savannah's busy riverfront. Among them was Jack Walters, a successful entrepreneur from London, who read: "This space features 150 feet of frontal property on the Savannah River and offers three commodious brick stores upon it fitted for counting rooms, and as receptacles for cotton, 3,000 bales of which may be conveniently stored therein."

Reading on, Walters was drawn by the next few sentences, which contained the following information: "The lot is a very central one and it is next adjoining the wharf where Minturn's Cotton Press is situated, which, of course, makes it more convenient for vessels taking in freight."

That ad would change the direction of Walters's brilliant business aspirations. After contacting the owner and committing to a legal lease of the property, he would establish a cotton warehouse at 313 River Street where he would contribute to the thriving worldwide market that was now headquartered in a city that appeared to be booming.

Opening his doors to prospective employees, he hired a towering vagrant named "Big Joe," whom he met while walking near the docked ships a few feet away. Joe would be his foreman and oversee the placement and storage of the cotton inventory. His hard work would assist Walters in converting his efforts to dollars.

Walters's enthusiasm was contagious as he dined with others who were thriving in the cotton business. And Big Joe wore a grin as wide as the river at having acquired a steady job under the reins of a successful businessman.

During the first few months, Walters established impressive contacts worldwide, and Big Joe was relieved to see that his job would remain permanent as the business succeeded beyond his imagination. For his efforts, Walters had given Joe a nook on the lower floor of the building where he could live in comfort and safety from the dangers of the streets. Sorting and stacking the bales of cotton was physical torture, and there was no one walking the streets of Savannah who could handle the challenge better than Big Joe.

One evening after Walters donned his top hat and left for an early dinner with his wife, Big Joe headed up the stairs to the warehouse to finish his day's work. About halfway up the stairs, he grabbed his chest. The pain was so intense that it spread through his shoulders, down his arms, finally into his heart.

Big Joe tumbled down the staircase to the bottom. When Walters returned the next morning, he found Joe's dead body sprawled across the floor.

Distraught by the loss of his laborer, Walters put his business on the market. After it sold, he and his wife boarded a ship and traveled back to London, grieving from the shocking sight of his once-smiling companion lying dead from unknown causes.

Cindy Lewis would be the first to confess that there was something strange going on in the upstairs storage room of her River Street restaurant called the Shrimp Factory.

It was 1977 when she opened the seafood eatery in a rustic old building that was once a cotton warehouse. Cindy had a grand time decorating the unique structure with authentic artwork and colorful accents. She started with wooden tables and round-backed chairs reminiscent of those on ships. Beautiful red-dyed linens dressed up the intimate dining rooms and added a touch of luxury to the rustic surroundings. She created nooks for private, romantic dining and dressed the original ballast (stone) walls with prints depicting the rich maritime history of the riverfront. On top of the decor, she shared secret recipes that generations of her family had passed down: a rich seafood bisque, massive crab cakes, and, of course, the Harrises' bananas Foster flambé, a favorite among Savannahians.

The Lewis family boasted an extraordinary reputation in the local restaurant industry. Successfully leading the market with their fresh seafood and luscious desserts, they also excelled in bringing their warm Southern charm, including their contagious smiles, to the dining tables of guests from all parts of the world.

In spite of all the good things going on at the Shrimp Factory, there's one unique difference that makes this restaurant with its iconic red-and-white awnings stand out from all the others. From the front door to the darkest corner of its vacant top floor, it is a place where *spirits* coexist with the people they come in contact with. And after nearly thirty years, it seems they aren't going away.

Cindy's first week as owner of the Shrimp Factory was filled with introductions to the paranormal coexisting in the area above the restaurant where liquor was stored. And she wasn't the only one. A dear friend named Joe had joined the staff. Healthy and strong, Joe adored the Lewis family as well as the new business venture.

One evening, shortly after dark, Joe went up the stairs to retrieve liquor at the request of the bartender. Halfway up the stairs, he missed a step and slid, traveling down the bumpy steps like a rag doll. He died later in the silence of the night, of a massive heart attack. Since he was in such perfect physical health, questions were put forth by his family: How could he have died of a heart attack? After all, he had never been sick in his life. Could someone or something have pushed him down the stairs? His sudden death was almost too shocking to accept. The questions would remain for years, and the memory of his loyal service would live long after his passing. His loss was indeed a blow to the family and the restaurant's patrons.

It shattered the soul of restaurant's owner. She began hearing voices coming from upstairs, as if a group were meeting there. At first Cindy believed the muffled sounds were coming from the crowds at street level who were marveling at the big ships that roll into port several times a day. But then she realized it wasn't the tourists who were making the fuss, but rather one voice, and at times several voices, upstairs. Perhaps these were Walters's former acquaintances reviewing their daily business agendas. Or perhaps it was a single soul talking to himself over and over. Regardless, the presence was carrying on its own agenda in the old brick building, and each time someone ventured up the stairs to retrieve supplies, that person was met with a cold burst of air halfway up and the feeling that someone was watching his or her every move.

At first Cindy blamed it on "coincidence," fearing that her strong cliché philosophy that "there's no such thing as ghosts" was merely being compromised by simple, explainable mishaps. Second-guessing the mysterious times when bottles crashed to the hardwood floor for no apparent reason, she finally succumbed to the fact that there was indeed a ghost, or ghosts, hanging out at the Shrimp Factory.

One evening as Cindy ventured up to retrieve some rum, she noticed the large keg dripping and the strong stench of liquor, as if a party were in progress. As she cleaned up the spill, she was consumed by the sensation of strong arms embracing her and the shallow breathing of something standing behind her. When she shared her experience with the staff, they too became fearful of climbing the stairs that were more than two hundred years old.

Janie sold the restaurant to her daughter the following year. That's when the new owner inherited a tolerable spiritual tenant who had no intentions of leaving.

One evening as her daughter opened the restaurant for dinner, the original heart-pine rafters began to tremble. There was seemingly a raucous gathering going on upstairs, and the noise appeared to indicate one of two events: a business meeting filled with the stomping feet of angry men, or a joyful celebration where toasts and celebrations dominated. As she stood near the cash register, all desire to solve the mystery vanished when a family of seven checked in for their reservation. She welcomed them with her glowing smile and let work consume her.

But that was just the beginning.

One day during the summer, supplies at the bar were running low. She spared her staff the task of interacting with a ghost and opted to climb the hot and humid stairs herself.

"As I slowly walked up the stairway, holding on to its wooden railing, scarred with random scratches, I passed through a wall of cold air. It actually felt quite good. There were times afterward that I walked up there for no reason. It actually felt refreshing, and I thanked my friend, the ghost, for reviving me," she said. She experienced this sensation on several occasions, reporting that the rush of cold air on her sweating body "always happens unexpectedly and in my experience, always after dark."

Accepting that the restaurant at 313 East River Street was officially haunted, she called an electrician in an attempt to prove or disprove her theory. The lights were flickering, and the fans were shutting off and on. In a building the age of hers, there were bound to be electrical issues.

Shortly before four in the afternoon, the electrician arrived, donning tools and gear to investigate the strange surges.

"Well, ma'am, I'm not a believer in ghosts, but I can't find anything wrong with your wiring," he reported after his inspection. "I'm going to send you an estimate to start from scratch and tear out all of the old work and replace it with the latest wiring and electrical technology, just to be sure. If you're willing to spend the extra money to get it right, I'll start right away."

She temporarily closed the restaurant, and after a week's worth of work, the project was completed. That night, she opened the doors for dinner and a worry-free evening doing what she loved best, smiling and chatting with all who entered the Shrimp Factory's door.

Around 8:30 p.m. the lights began to flicker, and by 10:00 the fans had become a nuisance. Although the electrician's estimate included brand-new dimmers and switches, nothing seemed to fix the mysterious electrical issues. Yet when other disturbances occur, such as glasses breaking and items flying off the shelves in the kitchen, "We continue to blame it on our ghost," she said, who has given up on any logical reasons for the unexplained happenings. "The meetings are still prevalent upstairs. The voices are plain and clear, and although there's a constant heated debate as to who our friend or friends really are, we all agree on one thing: His name was Joe, and he loved this old place."

The family sold the restaurant in 2013 and new owners Jennifer and Tim Strickland carry on the traditions started by the Savannah family in 1977. If you're visiting River Street on a hot muggy summer day, you may just enjoy a fresh brush of cold air if the Stricklands allow you to tour the establishment. We've heard that Old Joe is still at work and his arms are just as strong as they were when he caught the fall of the owner that first night as she climbed the stairs of The Shrimp Factory. He still loves the place.

THE BRIDE OF FORSYTH PARK

A mysterious shadow appears over hundreds of bridal portraits taken in beautiful Forsyth Park. Unknown to those who enjoy the park for recreation, the ghostly image of a shadowy bride takes on a lifelike image of legitimate wedding photographs with the fountain as a backdrop. This mystery bride is a sad woman who roams the thirty-acre park, possibly seeking the man who left her standing at the altar.

Savannah's lovely Forsyth Park is one of those outstanding rarities in the realm of the most beautiful places to visit in the world. Unfortunately, the city planners of the 1800s can't lay claim to creating the magnificence of this thirty-acre flourishing feast that nourishes outdoor enthusiasts.

A bit of city planning inspiration occurred in the 1850s when the wandering eyes of local Savannah administrators captured images of parks that were springing up all around the country. But the park prototype that most captured their fancy was not found in the United States, but rather in a part of the world with which few Savannahians were familiar: Paris, France.

The French demonstrated that the successful intermingling of flora and fauna with broad streets could affect a city's aesthetics in a most positive way. Beauty could be discovered in expansive boulevards that encircled splendid parks with monumental masterpieces placed in the center. And so, with a European template in hand, the first large park in the city was born.

Situated in the center of the city's acclaimed Historic District, Forsyth Park is bordered by Gaston Street to the north, Drayton Street (a one-way connecting road) to the east, Park Avenue on the south, and Whitaker Street (another one-way road) on the west. There is a lovely outdoor stage—a draw for all ages. There are a number of walking trails and a spray fountain where supervised children play in the summer heat, lending whimsy and joy to the outdoor haven. There is even a walled Fragrant Garden, built as a soul-soothing place for the blind to enjoy the scented splendors of spring. Fun, new outdoor eateries are within and near the park for consuming the area's vast and colorful landscaping.

Named for Georgia Governor John Forsyth in 1851, the park hosts magical outdoor festivals and concerts on a newly built band shell with a supporting amphitheater. But by all standards, the most breathtaking views can be experienced at the Gaston Street entrance, where the park's magnificent fountain can be best seen.

By far, the most outstanding feature of Forsyth Park is its fountain. In the shape of a two-tiered wedding cake, it offers a "robed female figure standing in extreme contraposition, holding a rod," according to the city's Park and Tree Commission, which oversees the maintenance. Acanthus leaves form the bottom layer of three rows of cast-iron leaves on the top basin that supports the figure. The pedestal holding up that top basin is magnificent and includes "grasses, cattails, and a wading bird with wings outspread." The basin stand is exceptional, with ornamental leaves. The water flows from sixteen pipes, and the bottom basin is itself a work of art, with spouting swans in the pool. An ornamental wrought-iron fence, which keeps people from tampering with the fountain, encircles the centerpiece of this flourishing park.

The fountain is not unique to the world of art. Its bears strikingly close resemblance to those found in the Place de la Concorde in Paris and in Cuzco, Peru. Renovated several times, the Forsyth Park fountain has become a symbol of Savannah's beauty and has been featured in films and TV shows.

Standing there and enjoying the portrait of live oaks cradling the grand fountain, flanked by azaleas that bloom in spring, one can only imagine that the broad sidewalk that leads to the center of the fountain was created as the most wondrous place for a bride to employ as her aisle. This is the place where her intricately laced train trails as she meets her groom and the priest at the wrought-iron gates directly in front of the fountain. Behind the wide trunks of the live oaks are romantic wooden park benches, where many a proposal has occurred.

The park is a scenic and delightful place for weddings and other joyful celebrations, along with family portraits. Sadly, it is also an eerie place for vagrants to camp on nights when shelters are full or too far to travel to by foot. And while the scene has been captured by wedding photographers' cameras for years, the thousands of images taken have resulted in one common conclusion: It is the fountain itself, and not the bride, that is the focus of each and every photograph.

The sprays of the fountain change color with the rising and setting of the sun. As the rays illuminate the droplets of water, shades of pink, purple, yellow, and green emerge like facets of a diamond illuminated by an ambient light.

The fountain would play a special part in the June wedding of a Savannah girl and her Alabama groom. With plans to schedule portraits in this idyllic setting, unbeknownst to the beaming couple, a bride jilted by her groom on the very apron of the fountain could put a damper on what would be an otherwise perfect wedding day.

Ammie and William's wedding day had been on the photographer's schedule for nearly a year. He realized the couple would be demanding, and although his inflated rates reflected his superb artistic perfection, he was concerned about a recurring shadow that was consuming every bride he photographed in front of the Forsyth Park fountain.

The shadow was positioned directly over each bride's gown and face, and no matter how much time he spent retouching, he could not remove it from the final portrait. His voice mail was filled with complaints from irate brides who had gone out of their way, in many cases traveling great distances, to wed in front of the monument. Although he had shared his woes with photography professors at the local art school, no one seemed to have a source or solution for this strange technical obstacle.

Ammie looked beautiful! Her wedding day was filled with last-minute preparations, and each one pointed to her ravishing appearance. First in line was the hairdresser, who would create an elegant updo that would frame her tiny face. William spent the morning golfing with his brothers and was busy taking care of his groomsmen's tuxedos and accessories. The church was filled with lilies and orchids, and the day was starting off as every bride-to-be would dream.

Ammie and William's wedding was to take place in a contemporary church on Wilmington Island, and its soaring ceilings and large expanses of glass would allow the beauty of the towering island pines to bring a fresh, outdoorsy feel to the interior of the sanctuary. The photographer could use "natural light," which meant that the photographs could be taken without flashes or strobes. He was hired to capture the couple's most intimate moments during the moving service, and with that in mind, he did it discreetly and tastefully.

Following the service that was attended by about three hundred guests, the photographer shot several portraits of the bride and groom, the wedding party, and their families, illuminated by the perfect cast of outdoor sunlight streaming in through the church windows. A trolley awaited the party outside to transport them to Forsyth Park, where he would shoot yet another round of photos near the ornate fountain.

He could feel the humidity rising as he hopped in his rusty blue 1999 Toyota, tossing his equipment carelessly into the backseat. Looking toward the sky, he could see a dark cloud moving in the direction of the Historic District. Hoping the rain would stay away, he raced to the park to get set up before the trolley arrived with the wedding party.

Parking about a half block away, the photographer trudged down the Gaston sidewalk toward the fountain, stopping short of a sight he did not expect. Leaning on the railing and looking into the spraying water was a beautiful bride, dressed in a gown that appeared to be from the 1920s. Her wavy hair seemed to be "oiled" into curls that wrapped her face. She was attractive and, in fact, reminded him of a character in a movie he enjoyed, *The Great Gatsby.*

"Hello, how are you?" he asked the tall, slender bride, who was holding a long-stemmed rose downward along the taper of her yellowed, lacey gown.

She was weeping, and he wasn't sure what to say. What he did realize was that a thunderous boom had just crashed, and a storm was about to ruin his shots in front of the fountain.

"I've been standing here for quite some time," she said. "Years, in fact."

Trying to decipher her intent, he backed away and set up his tripod. As he looked across the vast grassy field, he could see Ammie, William, and the wedding party racing toward the fountain, aware that at any moment the clouds were going to burst.

Losing the patience that he had arrived with, he left his camera setup and walked toward the woman, asking, "How can I help you?"

"On June 1, this very day," she replied, "my family and friends sat in simple white chairs along this sidewalk waiting for me to walk toward my lover, who would be standing in this very spot. We waited for several hours until the mosquitoes were driving us away and the night consumed a magnificent sunset. He never came, and since then I've taken it upon myself to see that brides who come here to wed are tarnished with my image—an image of happiness that I'll never know."

He was beginning to understand, and her tormented remarks suddenly struck a thought. The gray shadow that he had spent hours upon hours trying to remove from the bridal photographs taken at this exact spot was she!

"Just because you were jilted is no reason to ruin the happiness of other brides," he said sternly while the dark cloud hung directly over him. "You must settle this trouble within your soul and leave so that others might savor the joy of this ravishing monument."

Screaming with laughter, Ammie held her gown while continuing to run with her party. As they grew closer to the fountain, the mysterious bride turned, head down, and walked away into the thick brush, disappearing like fog in the early morning sun.

Realizing that he was fighting not one but two elements for his only chance to shoot Ammie and William near the fountain's spray, he ordered them to compose themselves and stand still—in spite of their giggling—like figures on a cake for his quick shot. As he snapped the shutter, giant drops of rain began to fall in big splats onto the sidewalk.

"We've got to get back on the trolley," Ammie said, laughing at the same time. "Let's just forget this. It's not worth getting soaked." They ran for the trolley, and it pulled away, loaded with the jovial wedding party. Meanwhile, the wedding photographer made it back to his ugly, dated, and inappropriate car filled with photo equipment and a half-eaten hamburger. He hoped no one saw him as he settled into the torn seat in a rented tuxedo. Checking the image on his camera as the trolley breezed by, he smiled.

In one hasty moment under the threat of a major rainstorm, he had captured a perfect picture of Ammie's gleaming white teeth, splendid veil, and handsome groom, as well as the bridesmaids and groomsmen, all standing around the glorious fountain at Forsyth Park. As he started the engine to drive away, the skies burst with thick rain.

Would the mysterious woman return to ruin the perfect wedding day for other Savannah brides? He had no way of knowing. But what he did know was this: The bride of Forsyth Park would never again stand in the image of *his* wedding clients.

117 LINCOLN STREET

It was a simple purchase for a man of his age and stature. But the two-bedroom condo in the Historic District of Savannah was something that most guys his age wouldn't touch. There was something strange about this condo that wouldn't be revealed until its new owner moved comfortably in, and then he would be forced to deal with eerie events unlike any he had ever experienced.

Traveling south on Lincoln Street, one might not even notice the stately red brick building that stands off the narrow sidewalk, much less its spooky inhabitants that have lurked inside throughout its history. Marked by its humble black umbrella-shaped awning, the apartment-style building is simple and reflective of its time period. Built in 1918 for an unknown owner, the structure appeared out of the downtown's sparsely staged area in the heat of a pandemic that killed hundreds in the city.

Today, little has changed about the facade at 117 Lincoln. Apartments inside have become trendy (and costly) condos and have retained their modest appearance. Some still offer street views with small rectangular-shaped balconies that overlook the charming one-way thoroughfare.

On the porch of Unit #5-A, humble furnishings included a plastic Adirondack chair and two medium-size pots, one filled with rosemary and the other with thyme, but it proved to be adequate decoration for the handsome and fit twenty-something newspaper reporter.

There was something classy about his new home, and Gene couldn't wait to use his key for the first time. Hitting the automatic dial that called upstairs, just for fun, the young writer skipped a few steps as he bounced up to the second story. He was officially the proud owner! Although the handsome space needed renovating, he felt an overwhelming sense of achievement for surviving his first closing. With the professionalism of a real estate mogul, he breezed through the mounds of documents to be signed that officially legalized the sale of the two-bedroom, one-bath condo in a prime area of the Historic District.

It felt almost as though he had won a million dollars, and when he walked through the front door for the first time and fell onto the well-worn couch his sister had donated, he began planning for an enlargement of the tiny galley kitchen by tearing out walls. After that, he would replace the filthy tile in the bathroom to his own taste.

"Gene Downs, Islands Close-up reporter for the *Savannah Morning News,* is now a homeowner," he joked to himself, imagining that particular headline appearing in bold letters across the front page of the next day's paper. He would certainly have to acquire some extra copies from the pressroom to send home to his family.

There was no doubt that he was excited, and the condo's "classiness" was seeping out into the living room and onto his meager balcony. "Wow," he thought as he gazed upward at the fourteen-foot ceilings framed with several layers of molding. This classy townhome had heart-pine floors with planks as wide as his two hands spread side by side, and all the doors and fixtures were original. He marveled at the thought of someone in the early 1900s physically laying the hand-cut planks.

"Ahhhhhh, I am a man blessed beyond my dreams," he thought jokingly, as if he were on a television sitcom.

Ensconced in the three-story building that was constructed as apartments in 1923, he was convinced that he would never move again for the remainder of his life. After all, what reason could he possibly imagine that would make him want to leave this humble but charming abode?

Almost speaking aloud, he mimed his first, best-selling novel on the coffee table, pounding out the keys with his slender fingers: "Coolness: defined in a single condo."

Night one.

The energetic reporter had withered to exhaustion with the deadlines of the day. He decided to call it done around 9:00 p.m., as he had taken the two previous days off to move. Tomorrow's schedule called for an early interview with an artist named Barbara Berry from Tybee Island, who painted seagulls in varying sizes and shapes. It wasn't exactly the news story he would have chosen, but his editor was a demanding and driven supervisor who was challenged by a twenty-four-page weekly to fill and a single reporter to help her do so. She knew that Gene wrote descriptively, and most of his articles could fill an entire six-column newspaper page. Besides, if it were a wee bit short, she could enlarge the seagull paintings to fill space.

Cuddling with his *New York Times,* he fell asleep quickly, and was awakened early the next morning by the thunderous sound of a massive garbage truck lifting a container full of the building's trash just beneath his bedroom window. So much for oversleeping, he thought. That'll never happen in this apartment. He chalked up the earth-shattering experience to the condo's outstanding "character," avoiding any negativity that might spoil his morning.

After a quick shower and shave, he stood at the bathroom mirror to brush his teeth. Staring into the glass, he suddenly felt as though someone were watching him. Seconds later, he heard someone calling his name, "Gene . . . Gene." The voice grew faint, and he almost dropped his toothbrush.

The little voice inside his head was whispering again incessantly, and behind the reflection of his face he could glimpse a hallway that made him physically sick. He feared that if he viewed it directly, something might jump out of the walls and into his path. If he glanced to the side of his face, he might actually see a person.

Had someone entered his home without a key? Had he checked the closets the night before?

His mouthful of toothpaste was by now swishing around like suds in a dishwasher as his mind raced. "What to do, what to do, what to do?" Could there be someone actually standing there? He decided he'd rather not know. After he finished rinsing and wiping the excess toothpaste off his mouth with the inside of his shirt collar, he headed down the hallway toward the front door. It felt as though he had to squeeze by to get past a human being that he couldn't even see standing there.

Gene quickly exited the condo, secured his backpack, and hopped on the bike that would take him a few blocks west to the newspaper building. After pedaling faster and faster, motivated by fear, he landed in the parking lot of the newspaper building, where he met some colleagues who were arriving for work.

"Hey, Gene! How's the move going?"

Wondering if he had made a huge mistake, he responded with a simple "Great."

Gene's to-do list was expanding. With renovation on his mind, he headed to the local hardware store, a downtown fixture for more than fifty years. He purchased a sledgehammer and biked two blocks to the gym, balancing the hammer on his handlebars. He would get in a quick workout before settling in for a night of demolition. Speedily riding past Joe Bean's—a quirky coffee shop on York Street—he suddenly put on the brakes. A colorful contemporary painting had caught his eye, and he decided to go inside and inquire.

He pictured the painting over his shabby sofa. It was indeed an adrenaline rush for this pauper who was now an official homeowner. The painting of the Dalmatian-mix dog with its unevenly spread spots and distinguished pose would add life and style to the condo.

"Can you tell me how I can get in touch with the artist?" Gene asked.

"The artwork was created by a talented young painter from Hilton Head," the guy at the counter said. "You can give him a ring. His name is Lenny Zimmerman."

Excited about the potential upscale addition to his new place, Gene headed back home, bouncing up the stairs as though he were entering again for the first time. Dialing the artist's number, he anxiously waited for what seemed like several minutes before someone answered.

"Hello, this is Lenny."

"Hi, my name is Gene Downs, and I recently bought a condo in downtown Savannah. I think your Dalmation painting would be awesome over my sofa. How much is it?" he asked, praying that it would be within his budget that was getting smaller every day.

"It's a hundred dollars," Lenny responded.

"I'll take it," Liam said gleefully. "I do have a slight problem, though. I don't have a car. Is there any way you could deliver it to my condo? I live downtown on Lincoln Street."

"What's your address?"

"One hundred seventeen," Gene answered, adding the specific directions.

"I know *exactly* where that is," Lenny said in a rather shaky voice. "I used to live there."

When the ringer in Gene's apartment buzzed, announcing Lenny's arrival, he opened the front door and invited him up the stairs to his new abode. As the artist entered the room, he looked around and said, "I painted this piece right here in this dining room." It was an uncanny announcement, but Gene took it as a sign that the sale was meant to be. The painting was, in a sense, coming home.

And besides, compared to the seagull paintings he had just written about for the newspaper, this was "true" art.

Lenny began reminiscing. He described his former residence as a dorm-like place that was owned by the Savannah College of Art and Design at the time. Three art majors lived in the apartment, and his room was in the very center of the space, which was now the open dining room.

"I had some weird experiences when I lived here," he said to Gene. "One night as I slept in this really skinny twin bed, I was awakened by someone walking across the floor. It sounded like he was walking on paper, but when I turned the lights on, there was nothing there."

Lenny said he shared his experience with his roommates, who accused him of having a bad dream. And then he continued.

"We used to have a big-framed Coca-Cola sign on that mantel up there," he said, pointing to the place that lacked Gene's proper staging elements. "In front of the framed piece, we had several old bottles that we had collected. We were standing on the balcony talking one evening, and all of a sudden, we heard a big crash. When we entered the room, lying on the floor, face up, was the smashed remains of the Coke sign. Glass was everywhere. Standing upright on the mantel were the bottles, untouched. Something literally lifted that picture up and threw it down on the floor in defiance and anger." Lenny said it wasn't long before the three roommates found someplace else to live.

After Lenny departed, Gene hung his new picture over the couch and stood back, admiring its impact on the room. Things were starting to come together, and it was time to start taking out that kitchen wall. Having warned the other residents that there would be some banging going on that night, he began slaughtering the tiny kitchen wall like a madman. When the last piece of plastered wall was lying on his floor in a crumbled mess, he went to bed, clutching his *New York Times*.

The next day, Lenny called.

"I forgot to tell you something last night," he said. "One evening as I was getting ready to go out for a night on the town, I was standing in the bathroom brushing my teeth. I thought I heard my name called, so I paused to see if it was one of the guys. No one answered, so I took a stroll around the house to no avail. I definitely think that place is haunted."

"Oh, great," Gene said, flipping through his mobile phone to find a psychic that he had met in the coffee shop.

The psychic's name was Lynn, and Gene arranged for her to spend the night on the worn-out couch beneath the Lenny Zimmerman painting. There was just one problem: It would be weeks before she could come. Savannah is a city where nearly every historic building has some type of active supernatural phenomena, and the psychic business was booming that spring.

So he went about his renovation projects with a vigor of Superman. He opened the kitchen up to the living room, painted all the walls, replaced the appliances, and retiled the bathroom. He felt completely satisfied by the time it was all completed.

One evening, the buzzer sounded. He dashed to the door to find Lynn, the psychic, finally arriving, bearing "tools": a candle and a recorder. She sat cross-legged on the floor, and Gene watched her intently, afraid that her clairvoyance might actually be legitimate. For four hours they attempted to reach "the being," finally giving up at around 4:00 a.m. Gene went to bed with all intentions of reading the *New York Times* that he had unknowingly clasped for the past three hours. Instead, he quickly fell asleep and was rudely awakened by the familiar grinding sound of the annoying garbage truck.

"Over time, after a complete renovation is accomplished," Lynn said, "the spirits will depart."

Satisfied with her answer, Gene cooked the psychic breakfast: scrambled eggs, sausage, and biscuits. After she departed, he went on to live "happily ever after," without so much as a glimmer from the ghost who had shown himself in various ways and through various mediums and to various residents at 117 Lincoln Street.

THE CONFESSIONS OF ANNA

The ghost of Anna Powers has endured centuries' worth of notoriety. The tragic tale of her death by suicide in the quaint inn called 17Hundred90 has been questioned and explored by historians and curiosity seekers. Did she die after throwing herself out of her bedroom window, or did her husband, who was said to be an adulterer, push her? Was it Anna who shoved her husband's mistress out the window? Or, could there be a twist to this story that changes the way Anna is perceived forever? One visitor discovered what really occurred at the inn while walking along the Savannah riverfront. Quite accidentally, the story of Anna's demise turned out to be a sweet surprise.

Marie Hutton, an accountant from Atlanta, searched online for the story of Anna Powers, the ghost that haunts the 17Hundred90 Inn. Her weekend getaway in Savannah was coming up, and she had booked a room at an inn that was known as being the home to one of the city's most highly publicized ghosts. She had already spent several hours on her computer researching records from the *Savannah Morning News*, but the name Anna Powers, with the words *suicide* or *murder,* never appeared in ink during those early years after the city was founded.

Marie set forth a personal challenge for her three-day stay. She was going to seek out Anna and astonish her peers back at work on Monday. She selected Anna because she had a few things in common with this spirit, such as they were both single.

Proving (or disproving) a legend would be a challenging break from her numbers job. But Marie realized that the odds were poor for catching a ghost and then having a face-to-face conversation with one.

Attractive and well dressed, Marie was also in excellent physical shape. She spent both time and money maintaining her appearance. Her job teaching aerobics two evenings a week kept her slim, and the extra money she earned allowed her to complement her physique with brand-name clothes and cosmetics, which she purchased from a high-end Buckhead boutique. However, although she seemingly had a lot going her way, Marie was lonely. She had endured her share of bad blind dates after breaking up with a man she had adored for ten years. Now she was approaching forty and still wondering if Mr. Right existed. But there were times when she would rather be alone than with a mismatched companion, and this weekend was one of those times. So instead of enjoying the warm sun of the Caribbean on a cheap cruise, she opted for a weekend in Savannah, where she could partake of a truly enchanting atmosphere, dine in extraordinary restaurants, and search out the supernatural.

The tales of Anna Powers were conflicting. According to one tragic legend, the ghostly figure so often seen by guests of the historic 17Hundred90 Inn was a forlorn woman who had lost her true love to the sea, and with a heart so shattered, she opened the second-story window and jumped out of Room 204 into the courtyard, plunging to her death.

Other versions of Anna's life and death still waft through the sultry Savannah streets, spilling onto the pages of shabbily written ghost books and cheap tours. Some say it was Anna who orchestrated the murder of her husband's mistress and that the figure who is seen through the window of Room 204 is an obsessed and angry woman who is filled with hatred and revenge.

Neither story had been accepted or proven—that is, until Marie's revelation.

The year 1790 was one of Savannah's most politically impacting. A council-mayor structure of government was set in place. More and more settlers were landing on the shores of the Savannah River in search of work and new opportunities. The location of the inn and the general layout of the two buildings strongly indicate that it was a boardinghouse, and assuming Anna was on one of the ships that sailed over, guesses are that she would become a permanent resident there. After all, it was affordable and convenient to the riverfront, where she may have hoped to find employment in the cotton warehouses.

Marie checked into the inn on Friday afternoon with the perception that she might immediately sense Anna's presence. Maybe she would feel her spirit tug at her sweater, hold her hand, or gently shove her down the stairs.

After she freshened up, Marie headed down to the bar, by now radiating a glowing ambience that was enhanced by the room's dimmed lights and strategically placed lanterns. She settled into a comfortable love seat, ordered a glass of wine, and glanced around. Within the realms of her mind, she began to pray silently that the spirit of Anna would appear. Maybe she would recognize her in an orb above the bar. Or perhaps she would see her face reflected in the old nautical mirror hanging over the fireplace. Better yet, maybe it would be Anna who would usher her to a table in the dining room.

One glass of wine turned to two, and within the hour her appetite grew, craving the fresh seafood entrees she had read about in *Atlanta* magazine's travel article on Savannah restaurants. And how she adored the 17Hundred90's restaurant! A massive fireplace illuminated the dining area, and her table in the rear allowed her to view the entire brick-walled room. Here she could seek to discover the suspicious shadows of Anna.

By 8:00 p.m., as Marie savored the last bite of fresh grouper covered in a light crust of pecan, she settled back, thinking of Anna and imagining how she could have been possessed to jump out of a window at least two stories high. Following dessert, she strolled outside around the structure and looked up into the window of Room 204.

She could hardly fathom the image she saw peering out the curtain in the window. Someone had placed a dummy of a tall woman in a see-through white gown in the window. She had to laugh.

A trolley tour paused beneath the window on the street, and Marie could hear the guide discussing Anna's fate as she pointed up to the figure in the window. Some of the patrons on the trolley stretched out the wide windows for a better view, snapping pictures and squealing. Some even shed a tear, openly wiping their eyes as the guide shared the tragic story of the woman who threw herself out the window.

Enough said. She was wasting her time looking for something that probably never existed.

Marie crossed Bay Street on foot and ventured down the treacherous ballast stones to River Street. She had read in a guidebook that walking on ballast was not something a high-heeled woman should do, and as she tried, she felt all eyes on her, watching her stumble and slide down. Her pathway was straight in front of the 17Hundred90 Inn. As she made her way down toward the river, she discovered a vacant bench and decided it would be the perfect spot to enjoy the view of the river while removing her heels and recovering from the venture down the hill. The chill of a late-winter frost touched her cheeks. In the distance, she could vaguely hear the booming sound of a ship blasting its horn. Perhaps it was coming her way.

It wasn't long before she noticed a beautiful woman dressed in a flowing floral gown coming toward her. With a satchel slung over her shoulder, she walked slowly, staring at Marie as she continued weaving a sweetgrass flower. Marie dug deeply into the pockets of her jacket. She was digging for change in her jacket when she realized she had forgotten her purse.

The woman was stunning, with long brown hair that fell to her waist and a flawlessly sweet face illuminated by the moonlight. She had a natural beauty without makeup and her hourglass, youthful figure was silhouetted and seen through her thin, white gown. Marie felt overdressed in comparison. She thought of the time she had spent earlier that evening prepping for her date with herself and dinner at 17Hundred90. In contrast, she didn't recall having ever seen such a naturally beautiful young woman.

Humbly walking over to Marie, the woman seemed shy and perhaps lonely. She turned to Marie and asked softly, "Do you mind if a poor girl sits for a minute of rest?"

The two looked at each other as if they were old friends.

"I come here so I can watch the ships as they enter the port," the woman said. "I've been coming here for years. It's really beautiful when they glide by filled with cargo. Sometimes you can see sailors standing along the bow.

"I was engaged to be married once, and I bade my love farewell just a few feet from here as he left to venture out to sea. Are you married?"

Marie paused for a moment and then answered with a smile, "I'm married to myself. There is no better companion."

The woman smiled and took the woven strands of sweetgrass that now formed a rose and placed it in her satchel. Her floral creations differed from those of the other roaming vendors. Within the varying shades of green in the stalks of sweetgrass was a single strand of red. It was her trademark, and most people who bought flowers from her recognized the extra care and color she added to the long-stemmed rose-shaped woven grass.

They sat silently for a few minutes, allowing a family and then a couple to stroll by.

The woman then turned to Marie and said, "People mock me."

"Oh, I'm sorry. I don't understand why they would do such a cruel thing."

"Yes. They come into my room disrupting my peaceful domain. They laugh and taunt and take pictures of my precious belongings. Every time something negative happens, they blame me.

"That's why I come here. I come here to feel the wind that perhaps is the same wind that blows across the sea and brushes the face of my lover. I come here to breathe the salt of the air that might find its way to the air that my lover breathes. I come here to be near him, even though I realize that he may be far away, never to return. I come here to watch the ships, hoping that he will be standing aboard, reaching out to me."

Marie watched as she gently took another long strand of the aromatic grass and joined it with two others, as though she were creating a French braid with long locks of a little girl's hair. Her sweetgrass roses offered stems that were long, like her thin, elongated fingers.

It was obvious by the swiftness of her creation that she had been hard at work weaving flowers for several years. She was quiet, gentle, and humble. Marie recalled watching the vendors in Charleston making much larger items from sweetgrass. None were as beautiful or as mysterious as this woman's.

It was getting late, and Marie had been warned not to walk the streets of Savannah at night alone. But a ship was getting closer, and she and her new friend were anxious as it glided up the river. They were almost parallel to the vessel, a cargo-laden ship heading to the terminal to be unloaded.

"Isn't it beautiful? Just look at the majestic bow and the massive beam. If only he were there," the woman said.

In spite of the scene, she never stopped weaving and by now was on her third flower. Within a few minutes, she would have a bouquet.

"They have me all wrong," the woman continued. "They don't understand. I wouldn't cause harm to anyone, nor would I harm myself. I just want to find him. I am holding out for the hope that we can be together one day. That is my only dream."

And with that, she stood and gracefully walked away, disappearing into the fog that had rolled up onto the River Street sidewalks.

Marie began her trek back to the inn. She had wanted to reserve "Anna's Room," but according to the reservationist, that room was booked months in advance by ghost-seeking tourists.

It had been a splendid night, and although her quest to meet a ghost might have been fruitless and would leave her one vacation day less, she had experienced the beauty of the wonderful place that was perhaps the boardinghouse where Anna had lived. She had dined on Savannah's famous seafood, and she had made a new friend who wove roses from sweetgrass.

The concierge was still sitting at the desk in the lobby, and Marie stopped to chat. Then, she headed down the carpeted hallway to her room.

As she opened the door, she felt a draft from the open window. The sheer draperies were blowing. On her bed was a woven sweetgrass rose with a single strand of red. Beside it, scratched in blue ink on a torn piece of yellowed vellum, were the words THANK YOU. ANNA.

THE MOON RIVER BREWING COMPANY

Savannah's only microbrewery has been championed by the world's foremost paranormal experts as well as by plain old fans of the establishment's beer. What this bar's patrons have discovered promises to keep you up at night.

On cold winter nights, the patrons of the Moon River Brewing Company will brave the chill to stand in line outside for a table or a seat around the bar. Once inside and cozy, they are overwhelmed by the warm ambience reflected in the bar's decor. There are authentic brick walls, dark pine floors, original English pub tables, and best of all, beers on tap varying in color from dark brown to deep amber to golden yellow, flowing into pint-size glasses.

Guests are always greeted by a host of waiters and waitresses who are loyal and long-standing employees of the bar, and most of the patrons know them by name. They are devoted to the establishment and range from college dropouts and struggling musicians to graduate assistants and medical students trying to bring home enough tips to pay the rent.

They are not just waitstaff, but experts trained in describing the various flavors found in the meticulously brewed beer. Their loyalty to the bar's owner and brewmaster, John Pinkerton, is a sure sign of success for a business housed in a building that is nearly two hundred years old, and Pinkerton himself is often seen floating in and out of the glassed-in room where the beer is brewed. Occasionally he'll make the rounds, coaxing reviews of his work from patrons sipping the brew.

There are a few traditions at the Moon River. Fridays at five o'clock, the brewmaster will signal the crowd and salute the end of the workweek in a rousing toast. Nightly rituals are common too, and special occasions from birthdays to marriage proposals are heralded in cheers throughout each evening. At times the mix of conversation will escalate to extreme noise levels from jovial groups of patrons who stroll in for a brew and camaraderie. After all, a raucous atmosphere is a sure sign of a great pub.

Aside from the atmosphere and the food, the biggest attraction at the Moon River brewery is its beer. Beer connoisseurs have heralded SavannahFest, a German-style microbrew and the trademark of the brewery, and it has put the establishment in the pages of newspapers around the country. With its orange hue and rich flavor, patrons consume barrels of it year-round. Other Moon River beers have been equally applauded.

On occasion a group of tourists and their guide from the "Haunted Pub Crawl" and other ghost tours will barge in the already packed establishment, climb the stairs to the dark and gloomy floors above, and with beers in hand, enjoy a microbrew mixed with a little paranormal activity on the side. Indeed, the brewery is one of those Savannah places where the facts have been proven: One can feel both giddy and scared at the same time. For, you see, the Moon River Brewing Company is haunted beyond comparison. There are so many spirits walking in and out of the building, both seen and unseen, that enumerating them has become a challenge and even a survival technique for those who work there, and they have even attracted some internationally known ghost hunters.

In 2009, the Travel Channel explored the cellar with video and audio equipment. The dark, cold room was slightly illuminated by a flashlight, and early on a voice was recorded saying the words, "It's the god, it's the god."

For the past eight years, Christopher Lewis, the operations manager at Moon River, has survived so many close encounters that one might surmise that he should either retire or quit soon. One recent evening while he was working in his office, he froze as a "being" walked right past him. The shadow was silent, and the encounter was brief, but it was enough to remind Lewis that he should never, ever be completely alone in the brewery. Often, items such as glass bottles have literally flown by him, forcing him out the door in fright, leaving his mounds of paperwork on the desk. When morning comes and he checks back in for the day, he'll discover that many of his personal items have been moved or hidden. Could this be the work of a child? After all, he has heard a child's laughter when there were no children in the bar.

There's a colorful and shady history behind the popular Savannah landmark. If you stand in the front entranceway and stare into the bar, your view of the check-in desk will become a vivid image, almost like you're overcome with a strong sense of déjà vu. The structure was the city's first hotel, appropriately named the City Hotel. Opened in 1821, it enjoyed a short run doubling as a post office and bank. After the hotel closed just four years after it opened, it became a coal warehouse, followed by a successful run as an office-supply store.

Reminiscent of the old hotels in cowboy movies, the wooden stairs that lead up to what were once guest rooms are unfinished and rough with age. The floors are dusty, and some doors hang off their hinges. Fully renovating the building would dig so deeply into the pocketbook of its owners that much of it is left unchanged, with only a new roof to protect it from the elements.

When Hurricane David destroyed many parts of Savannah in 1979, the roof was blown off, and the building that once hosted some of the 1800s most distinguished guests was shattered, ruined, and moldy. A brewery opened shortly thereafter, and renovations were under way. But when spirits began revealing themselves to workers, it closed, leaving construction at a standstill.

When Pinkerton and his partner purchased the building, they had their work cut out for them. Determined, however, to see the construction completed, Moon River finally opened to the raves of beer fans. The upstairs, left undisturbed, is the area most influenced by the supernatural, so much so that several television shows have filmed episodes at the brewpub, claiming that cold spots abound throughout the old hotel.

The night was young when Christine and her friends from college settled in around the bar for the ritual of the Friday toast. Ordering their favorite brews, they seemed to be talking over each other, sharing news and discussing where to catch dinner. As the bartender sat the pint glasses on the old wooden bar, wiping up the spillage, the group's attention was drawn toward the rear. A woman dressed in a period costume entered through the closed and chained back door. She was walking straight toward them. The bartender's eyes never left the figure and the girls sat frozen, amazed that the strange vapor-like figure was moving their way. The woman took a seat at the end of the bar between two empty stools, but before the bartender could ask her for her order, she disappeared.

Forgetting all about their beers, with foamy heads that were disintegrating, the girls tried to make sense of the scene that had broken up their conversation.

"Did you see that? Oh my gosh! Who was that? *What* was that? Was it a ghost? Are there ghosts here?" Christine exclaimed, hardly able to speak the words.

The bartender, who was still startled, said simply, "Yes. There are ghosts here. Let me tell you about Toby.

"As with most ghosts who refuse to leave Savannah's haunted dwellings, we've named ours. His name is Toby, and he appears at the most unlikely times. Although he isn't harmful, he can starkly remind you that he is still in charge. Just the other night, I had finished wrapping the silverware in linens and marked each spot at this bar with a set. When I turned around to serve a patron, Toby went into action. After I served the beer, I turned to see a set of the wrapped silverware sliding down the bar and pushing the others to the end. I wouldn't be telling you this if someone else hadn't seen it too."

The girls decided to stay and order from the menu. After all, they had seen a ghost, and chances were that they would soon see another one.

Christine slipped off her bar stool and slowly walked toward the restroom at the back of the restaurant. As she strolled, she looked up the stairway and met the eyes of a woman dressed in a white flowing gown, as if she were headed to a ball.

"Yikes. I think that was another one," Christine mumbled.

When she looked up the stairs again on her way back to the bar, she saw nothing. Back at the bar, she shared what she had seen with the bartender.

"I hate to tell you but, yes, we've seen her too."

Brewmaster Pinkerton was making the rounds and stopped by the bar to check on the girls. "Everything going OK here? Enjoying your beer?"

The girls looked at Christine as their "official" spokesperson.

"Well," she replied, "everything we've read or heard about this place is true. Tonight we've seen two ghosts: a woman who entered the back door and sat at the bar with us, and another who was dressed for a fancy party. Now, can you tell us if anything else will happen before we leave? It's getting late."

Pinkerton smiled, pleased that he could add the girls to his long list of ghost-spotters. The Syfy channel was next in line and had arrived to set up cameras, hoping to spot the woman on the staircase. They weren't successful. Yet, these unassuming girls who had gathered for a night of fun at his brewery were the ones she chose to reveal herself to. As for the woman entering the back door, that was a new one. Pinkerton could hardly wait for the next ghost to be revealed. Perhaps he could serve him or her a pint of his special brew. And perhaps the same spirit would return for more.

A logical guess would get him nowhere. He voiced his thoughts loudly over the crowd noise.

"Nothing is logical in this place."

And with that, he poured himself a beer.

TYBEE'S 12TH TERRACE GHOST

In the South, the corrective eye of a grandmother can become a haunting reminder of the importance of good behavior.

For sisters Jean and Jan, spending time at Nana's beach house along the shores of Tybee Island was a summer ritual they enjoyed and, secretly, sometimes dreaded.

Apart from the fun stuff like hanging out at the arcade, riding the Ferris wheel on the south beach, eating snow cones, and crabbing along the Back River, they spent a month every year learning about society's strict social graces from their nana. After all, one day they would be making their debut in beautiful ball gowns with other Savannah high-society darlings.

She taught them that every young woman should learn to play bridge and she spent hours dealing cards and explaining the definitions for terms like trump, pass, and bid. She showed them how to properly cut meat at the table and to use tiny little bowls with tinier glass spoons to salt their food. They learned the proper way to place a napkin in their lap and how to cover their mouths when coughing.

In the evenings, she taught them to set tables with varying silverware, pass the food in the right direction, and to never, ever, answer an adult without saying, "ma'am" or "sir."

When the day's lessons were over, the girls traipsed downstairs to their beach club, a two-bedroom hideaway where they played spades as if they were adult ladies at a bridge club, sometimes wearing the pink lipstick they took out of Nana's pocketbook. When Nana started to miss them, she'd clip clop down the stairs and peek in, sometimes catching a glimpse of the girls playing, sitting in a sea of wet towels placed on rugs with footprints caked with sand.

"Those girls, ummmph," she would say as she shook her head.

When the card games turned to boredom, they headed out the door to the beach to the big swing that looked onto the waves, seagulls, and sunbathers. Sometimes, beachgoers could hear a shrill voice screaming, "Stop slamming the door," all the way to the water's edge.

Nana's beach house could be compared to a small estate, towering above the sand dunes that overlooked the Atlantic Ocean. The three-story brick house had massive porches at each level that slanted down so the water could run off the edges. The ceilings were painted haint blue, a color stolen from the Charlestonians who called it that first, a slang for the word "haunt."

Almost every porch in Charleston had a haint blue ceiling to ward off the evil spirits. Said to be the color of water, the ceilings likened a pool to divide good and evil as evil can't travel through water. When that word got back to Savannahians, porches began to take a haint turn all through the city and out to the beach at Tybee Island.

Through the years and summers spent at Tybee, the girls grew into beautiful young ladies who could curtsy, ballroom dance, and dine in the finest restaurants with perfect poise. Nana lived to be ninety, and one day, she simply passed away in her sleep as the sun rose through her bedroom window. After she was buried, the beach house was sold for almost a million dollars and a vacation rental company took it over as one of its most popular, and expensive, properties to stay in at the quirky beach called Tybee.

Forward to 1996 and the filming of a movie called *The Gingerbread Man*, directed by Robert Altman. Altman and crew bombarded Savannah with sets, actors, and actresses. Among the famous to stay for extended time periods were Kenneth Branagh, Robert Downey Jr., Tom Berenger, Daryl Hannah, and Robert Duvall. From the downtown squares and Historic District homes, Savannah became a hub for the movie set. Downey's assistant reached out to the Tybee Island home rental company for a house with a view of the ocean, a nice beachfront, and, better yet, lots of bedrooms for his guests. His choice happened to be a nice brick, three-story home set on 12th Terrace where two little girls would play, summer after summer.

For six months, Downey made the 15-minute drive out to Tybee after long days on the set. He hired a chef and hosted gatherings when filming was delayed. Tybee locals spotted him at the beach hangouts and jogging along the sand. They embraced stardom, which was frequent there, and they accepted the fact that as long as there were celebrities at Tybee, there would be a wild party or two.

On occasion, Downey invited his entourage to stay with him at 12th Terrace. At the end of the stay when the film had concluded its location work, his assistant was asked to fill out a comment card.

On behalf of Downey, he gave high marks for their comfortable stay and, in true Southern form, bragged on the cleanliness and space of the home. They checked the box that asked if they would stay there again. They agreed to recommend it to their friends. It was convenient to Tybee businesses and getting on and off the island was effortless. The review was five stars. However, there was one comment, a question, that stood out.

"Who is the woman who keeps screaming, 'Stop slamming the door'?"

THE HOUSE ON ST. JULIAN STREET

Savannah was a bustling business hub in the 1960s. The Historic District was vibrant and colorful. Gentlemen in corduroy slacks and plaid jackets dotted the streets with leather briefcases in tow, heading to the varying banks that anchored the four corners of Johnson Square. Ladies in tiny hats and A-line dresses sipped on tea in heart-shaped metal chairs that were positioned along the sidewalks of Broughton Street. Store fronts with fashionable outfits on curvy mannequins enticed shoppers and the counter at the Kress (five-and-dime) was elbow to elbow with hungry diners.

Sitting tilted and precariously on temporary wooden supports and in view of many who passed by, an oddly shaped barn-like home appeared as a dilapidated eyesore that seemed totally out of place in this stylish city. With some slats missing and others dangling from its framework, this was a home that was, indeed, teetering on disintegration. Right next to it was a single house of like architecture.

The house at 310 East Bryan Street was constructed in the late 1700s and later situated on a civic trust lot. It is said to be one of the oldest surviving houses in the Historic District of Savannah.

When it met the eyes of James Arthur "Jim" Williams in 1969, the downtown area had fully recovered from a centuries-old fire that consumed most of the beautiful Savannah homes. Strangely, this old structure and its accompanying smaller house were among only a few to survive that raging fire in 1796 that destroyed 226 properties and was appropriately named "Savannah's Great Fire."

On this day, its shabby framework was begging for attention. However, the current owner realized it was time for the old home to be laid to rest. So before he set to tear it down, he reached out to a debonair and highly respected gentleman and lover of fine old homes who just might just be interested in purchasing the remaining pieces of the interior wood.

Savannahian Jim Williams had a passion for preservation. Throughout his lifetime, he orchestrated the restoration of more than fifty homes in Georgia and South Carolina. From his early twenties, he was drawn to finding beauty in old homes. It became the driving force for his work that would change the landscape of Savannah and other properties in the land called "lowcountry" forever.

In old homes, Williams saw beyond the crumbling façades that hardly appeared to be worth saving. Instead of calling for demolition when he came upon a collapsing or deteriorating property, his visions were filled with fine fixtures and finishings, grand staircases, and handcrafted fireplaces. Once the work was completed, he created interior masterpieces complete with outdoor havens, magical gardens, glorious terraces, and floral wonderlands around stunning fountains that he purchased and had shipped from various parts of the world. He didn't stop there. Interiors were lavish with fine Oriental rugs and one-of-a-kind antiques he had shopped for in remote and exotic locations. Once he eyed a home project, if it didn't suit him with regard to its location, during the construction process, he would—assuming all, or some of the expense—have it moved to a more conducive location.

Williams didn't let anything get in his way. Once he set his eyes on a property that could, or should be, condemned, his first action was to pursue ownership and immediate protection from the wrecking ball. In all, he began his beautification journey in 1955, according to *Savannah's Jim Williams & His Southern Houses*, an elegant table-top book written by his late sister, Dorothy Willliams Kingery.

Kingery was inspired by her brother's talents and documented his progressive restorations in the pages of her detailed book, including the Hampton Lillibridge House.

Williams was only twenty-four years old when he started his beautification journey of restoring three dilapidated homes. His success quickly became the talk of the town. And while he was restoring houses from centuries-old remnants, he was also building a reputation as one of the foremost authorities on historic house restorations.

By the time his interest in the historic house on East Bryan appeared, his plan was already in action. Williams saw a pristine, quaint cottage-like home and imagined it being moved and resettled among the distinguished neighborhood homes that lined St. Julian Street, a much more desirable location several blocks away.

But what was it about this house that attracted Williams?

By most standards, it was junk and there was little worth salvaging. Could there be a spirit that subliminally tugged at his heart and led him to pursue this unique, abandoned, broken-down house? Or would someone, or something, block the steps to Williams's transformation? The answers would come in a series of strange occurrences that would take him on a supernatural journey that was both terrifying and dangerous.

As with all his projects, Williams researched the house he was thinking of buying and discovered that the original owner, Hampton Lillibridge, was a wealthy New Englander who had it built in 1796—the same year as the fire—in the style of Newport, Rhode Island, homes. History revealed that after the original owner died of yellow fever, his second wife sold the home and it was transformed into a boarding house.

His research also led him to some interesting architectural images that explained the uniquely northern-coast characteristics of the house. Lillibridge had decided to build an idyllic replica of his Newport-like home in Savannah from cypress clapboard, mirroring Rhode Island residences with a striking profile reminiscent of his own home's classic architecture.

With features that included a gambrel (or barnlike) roof, dormer windows, and a widow's walk—perfectly suited for ladies seeking a bird's-eye view of ships coming into the Savannah seaport—the home would enhance downtown's noble architectural heritage. Indeed, with Williams's masterful project management experience and interior design talents, the house would stand out once the restoration was completed. But nothing Williams ever did was easy, and several strange events led to the relocation of the structure to St. Julian Street that ended in the accidental deaths and a multitude of bizarre happenings.

Lillibridge's house sat next to a smaller house of similar design, and Williams was drawn to the pair of structures as they stood in the poorest of conditions so he acquired both.

Both the small and larger house were slated for demolition, but Williams had other plans. He would alert the Historic Savannah organization and, first on his agenda, stop the demolition. Then, he would work with the organization and the Port Society to relocate the houses from its Bryan Street location to nearby St. Julian Street, where the houses would be renovated and used as their headquarters. With the blessing of Historic Savannah, Williams initiated his plan to move the pair of houses to St. Julian Street. That's when the first tragedy struck.

During the much-publicized move, the second house collapsed and killed one of the workers. The others escaped injury when they slid into space in the floor where the former chimney had been. Discussions ensued between Williams and the architect, John C. LeBey. LeBey told Williams that both houses were unfit for restoration and recommended that the larger house be torn down completely, as the smaller house had already proven its weakened state. But Williams managed to convince him that the larger house could be saved and, after bracing the interior for the trip, successfully moved it through the streets of downtown Savannah to its final resting place. That afternoon, after all the workers had left the scene, Williams was about to leave when he heard a loud noise that he described as "a cracking sound." It was the sound of the entire back wall of the house collapsing, leaving only steel cables holding the walls upright. It was truly a sound that Williams should have taken as a warning to leave well enough alone.

Italian author Italo Calvino once said, "The more enlightened our houses are, the more their walls ooze ghosts," and if that is the case, Williams had his fair share of them.

In this house alone, Williams would awaken to someone standing at the foot of his bed and feelings of being embraced by someone wrapped in ice. Then there were beings hosting gatherings upstairs, a worker killed, and a host of other freakish events that continued while he lived there.

And this was just the beginning.

It was a humid afternoon in Savannah, the kind of day where the skin is frothy with sweat, even while sitting in the porch shade. There was a tenseness in the air. The workers reconstructing Williams's home on St. Julian Street were mentally stressed from fighting off his annoying poltergeists. Some were threatening to quit, and some had already walked off the job.

They were terrified of the sights and sounds that were coming from the centuries-old house Williams was paying them to restore.

As the Savannah heat changed to a frigid chill, Williams's patience was dwindling. He was losing sleep. His exhaustion was transformed into a distraction from his successful antiques business that he so enjoyed. The happenings at the St. Julian Street house that he had so lovingly and beautifully brought to life was destroying his hope for a peaceful and beautiful home.

So, in the Jim Williams style of seeking resolution, he set all his forces into action, calling on the services of a psychic he had first met in London.

Standing on the platform in front of the meager Savannah train station wearing a dark trench coat, Williams reached inside his coat's hidden pocket for his lighter. His cold fingers made it difficult to light in the strong and chilling breeze, but he finally held a flame on the third try. He glanced around nervously, questioning his rationalization with each puff. The tension was almost unbearable as he hadn't slept in days. His grand restoration project was a huge success but constantly being jeopardized. His crew was trying to complete a job, but between them and success stood unknown forces calling his efforts folly.

Williams finished the last puff, tossed the butt to the ground, and continued to second-guess his decision. After all, he was a man of great integrity. On the other hand, there was no place to go with the dilemma he couldn't solve by rational means. He had been told that when all chance, coincidence, pranksters, and rational explanations could be ruled out, it was time to call in a professional.

Williams was all about following the rules. Standing near the track, glancing northward for a glimmer of the incoming southbound train, he realized that it was too late to change his mind. Within minutes a world-famous psychic would be stepping off the train. And Williams, an Episcopalian, would be turning to the paranormal to solve the problems that couldn't be solved by the police, his prayers, or mere luck.

With the piercing sounds of the powerful brakes that seemed to shake the earth, the train came to an ear-shattering halt. Williams reached out to assist his guest down the stairs. Her luggage consisted of a small, lightweight floral-colored suitcase. Maybe her minimal personal belongings meant that the task at hand wouldn't take too long.

The windows of Williams's automobile were fogging up as he and his guest made their way around Savannah's squares and toward the Hampton-Lillibridge home. They were almost speaking over each other, the warm fog from their breath filling the windshield. He shared the story of the events leading up to that moment with his passenger in horrifyingly graphic detail that he had gone over in his mind a thousand times.

"As we were moving the smaller house, two men with sledgehammers knocked the supports from the back of the house. At once, this caused the structure to fall backward just a few days ago, a dangerous and frightening event occurred in the house as it was settling onto a foundation that we had prepped."

She continued to listen intently as he shared more:

"Nice work," Williams said to the crew as they reviewed the day's progress in the downstairs living room. "We've got to finish hanging the doors and installing the hardware, and I would appreciate it if you'd clean these floors so I can move in."

"At that moment strange footsteps, the sounds of chains dragging on the floor, laughter, and whispers from above stopped the group from continuing their work. It was as if someone was hosting a welcome party for Williams, only they weren't invited. And then it got worse.

"What's that noise?" asked Sam, a member of my construction team. "I'm going to see for myself."

As he reached the top floor, listening for voices, Sam felt as though he were being engulfed by a "pool of cold water" and the only way he could keep himself from falling down an open chimney shaft was to lie down at the shaft's edge. When his colleagues reached the top of the stairs, they found him lying facedown on the floor, shaking and crying.

"Something was pulling my body toward the open chimney shaft. I fought the strong tug and threw myself down on the floor, away from the opening. I felt as though I was going to be swallowed up," he told Williams.

The exorcist was stunned as he recounted.

After the incident the crew left for the night, and Williams stood outside and pondered his options, wondering if they would return the next day. All in all, his fears were mounting. To that date, the list of strange happenings was growing: a gentleman had hung himself prior to the move when the home was a boarding house, a friend of the previous owner had died of pneumonia and now, his workers were almost killed and one would soon die.

That morning around eleven, Williams drove up to check on his crew. As he stepped out of his car and walked toward the house, Preacher, his foreman, rushed to greet him, simultaneously talking and running away from the structure.

"Mr. Williams, that house over there is full of people that ain't working for you, and we are all leaving," he said.

"Tell me what's going on," Williams begged. But Preacher was already in his truck with the engine roaring and the gear in reverse, leaving Williams with only one choice.

So it was that just two weeks before Christmas, Williams and his priest, the Right Reverend Albert Rhett Stuart, stood in the home's drawing room. Throughout the rite of exorcism, Williams never flinched. For forty-five minutes, accompanied by his work crew, it seemed as though this time the spirits were outnumbered. A feeling of peace overwhelmed Williams and his guests as the priest commanded the evil spirits to leave. Concluding with a blessing of the house, the evening ended with toasts for a peaceful night. And for a while, the ceremonious exorcism by a Savannah priest seemed to work.

As Williams lay in bed that night, he slipped off into a restful and peaceful sleep as he had not had in months. And for a while, the exorcism—the only one ever recorded in Savannah—seemed to bury the evil spirits. However, the next day, the crew happily began their work anew, sanding floors and putting up paneling as if nothing had ever disturbed them.

Dame Sybil Leek was a flamboyant London socialite who catered to wealthy collectors like Williams. She and Williams met while he was on a shopping swing through England and stumbled across her shop. Short in stature and plump with dark brown hair that strayed in all directions, Dame Sybil fit the mold of a psychic.

She spoke in short, fragmented sentences in a high-pitched voice that was continuous and, at times, annoying.

A few weeks previously, she had just rolled out of bed when her phone rang. Williams was frantic, so she booked a flight immediately.

After the lengthy transatlantic flight to New York, she boarded a train and headed south to Savannah.

"Séances are our best way to communicate with the dead," Sybil said. "We need to find out who these people are before we can try to talk them into leaving you alone. We'll hold a séance as soon as I arrive."

It was a cold, raw, and rainy night—the kind of night when the elements discourage outings. Williams welcomed his two chilled, damp guests into his home, which was still undergoing renovation. Sybil the psychic centered a card table in front of the main foyer. After striking a match to light a thin candle, she instructed the threesome—Williams and his workers, Preacher and Sam—to remain quiet. They joined hands and as the wind whipped around the house, she took the lead, calling out for the spirits to reveal themselves. The three men listened intently, hoping that nothing would appear; they were convinced that her credentials would neutralize whatever evil being had taken up residence in the house.

Williams was cautiously optimistic for results. As he and Preacher stared at each other, waiting for something to happen, Williams nervously cleared his throat and he and Preacher almost laughed.

Sybil called out again, "Please show yourself! Who are you? Why do you dwell here?"

Voodoo aside, three grown men in need of a strong drink were becoming a trio of nervous and impatient doubters. And as the rain fell outside and the drops hit the tin roof like a horde of faraway drummers tapping out of sync, nothing happened.

Several hours passed and Sybil's neck was aching from the head-thrashing that accompanied her chants. Her voice was becoming raspy, and she could sense that the dead were probably just that. Dead. After several hours of chants and Williams's prompting, they decided to call it quits. Sybil reported feeling "the presence of a woman with children," and although her astounding theory was heard, it was a far cry from reality. So, Williams sent his psychic to New York by train and, from there, back to England.

That very next night, the spirits were back.

Long moans, whispering laughter, clanging glasses, and dragging chains lulled an exhausted Williams to sleep. Lying in bed in a deep slumber, he was startled by what he hoped was a dream or hallucination. It was 3:30 a.m., and there was someone, or something, in his room. Williams's voice sliced the darkness with authority.

"What do you want?" he growled. A sound like crunching sand filled the dark space as he lay in his bed, hardly breathing. As the sound continued, he saw what appeared to be a figure standing about four feet from his bed. Drenched in nervous sweat and frozen as still as a dead man, Williams watched intently as the figure ran toward the bedroom door. On its way there, it hit an open closet door before vanishing. For Williams, the bedside incident was enough to lead him to yet another attempt at cleansing his home of tormenting spirits.

This time, he hired professional psychic researchers from Duke University to study his strange happenings. And from séance to exorcism, nothing rattled the throng of unwanted ghostly guests while he kept residence.

Dr. William G. Roll, an Oxford-educated parapsychologist, then serving as Duke University's parapsychology department chair, was his next authority. Dr. Roll was highly educated and had investigated countless cases.

The beginning of the investigation consisted of a tedious round of questions in Dr. Roll's five-part feedback form that Williams reluctantly attempted to answer. The overview section asked for details regarding the situation, and if those details coincided with special events (birthdays, anniversaries, deaths), the facts could open doors. The questionnaire asked for specific dates and descriptions of the events. For instance, who was there and what happened? The final section asked if any of the recipients had ever been a part of poltergeist disturbances. After filling out the time-consuming questionnaire, it was determined that Williams was a candidate for a study that was worth a personal visit from Dr. Roll.

It has been said that Dr. Roll called Williams' Hampton-Lillibridge House, "the most psychically possessed house in the nation."

With weeks turning into months and activities still taunting him, Williams realized there was no other choice. He would call on his priest.

A few weeks later, while Williams sat reading in his meticulously furnished parlor, the noises began again. Moans were heard, and the top floor of the house seemed to be bursting with action: people talking, more metal dragging across the wooden floors above, music and laughter. It was that evening that Williams decided to move out and put a "For Sale" sign on the lawn.

Today, the home is occupied, and the residents retain their privacy. They claim to feel nothing but joy living in the house that they say is spirit-free, with the exception of various "feelings" that a female presence and perhaps children may still occasionally roam the top floors.

Just about every night, ghost tour groups stand on the sidewalk and gaze upward as their guide shares the home's frightening history. Sometimes the tourists will fixate on an upstairs window where every now and then a dark-haired man wearing a white shirt and black bowtie is seen peering out at them as they stand below on St. Julian Street.

The characters that molded the story have all passed away: Jim Williams died unexpectedly in 1990 following a media frenzy arising from the court trials that led to his acquittal for murder. His story was told in print and on the big screen in a film titled *Midnight in the Garden of Good and Evil.*

Although both Sybil Leek and the Reverend Stuart have passed on, their legacies remain in stories told and retold in Savannah. There are rumors of witchcraft is practiced today by a strong following of locals and at times, their chants can be heard in the dark alleys and vacant buildings of Savannah's Historic District. No other exorcism has been recorded in the city, at least on the record.

And while everything appears settled, there are still questions.

Were the spirits consuming the house during Williams's time there trying to communicate with him directly? Could they have attached themselves or to various architectural elements or even antiques that Williams had confiscated from other homes? According to Dr. William Cox, an investigator from the Institute for Parapsychology in Durham, North Carolina, "He [Williams] may himself have been more of a sensitive on the premises and very much in touch with these spirits."

Maybe he still is.

EPILOGUE

GHOSTS UNMENTIONED

This compilation of tales retold from the dark side of Savannah hasn't come without extensive research. Most of the facts you've read were actual parts of history that have been verified and meshed with stories told and retold by Savannahians. The fun part of the job included countless interviews for those stories told firsthand. I spent hundreds of hours in the basement of the Savannah Historical Society wearing white gloves required to carefully handle the original newspaper articles and documents that have been sealed in plastic. And now, this updated edition is refreshed by much of the same information available with the original documents online.

Although there are literally hundreds of ghost stories floating around the city, there is one drawback: there is not enough ink or space to capture them all in print. There are new stories literally, every day, created by ongoing encounters. My intentions from the start were to share some old stories in new ways that keep them fresh and interesting.

When I contacted a public relations representative at the Savannah College of Art and Design (SCAD) for the first edition, she revealed a fact that was not only astounding, but true for almost any structure in the Historic District and beyond: "Almost every building that SCAD owns in Savannah has a ghost, or ghosts, dwelling in it." After exploring many of the old buildings and conducting interviews with the owners, I can vouch that her comments are true. There's a ghost in almost every old building and private homes in the city of Savannah, and some who hang out on the streets.

Forgive me if this book has strayed from those stories that have been repeated and written about for many years. Those tales may be discovered on ghost tours in and around all parts of the city, including Savannah's south side and islands.

As another footnote, I've seen two ghosts during the course of writing this book. One came through the brick wall in the tavern at The Olde Pink House. Dressed pirate-like, he emerged grinning ear-to-ear, almost laughing with a gold front tooth shining, before vanishing in a second. The other was standing on the side of Highway 80 East in the shallow marshland on the side of the road as I was driving to Fort Pulaski. At first, I thought he was a reenactor dressed in full Confederate garb; however, at 10:00 a.m. on a weekday morning, I seriously doubt it. Keep in mind as you read, some names have been changed and ghost stories are in itself, fiction. With that said, it's been a joy scaring you.

Happy hauntings!

APPENDIX A

ORBS OF WISDOM

Research is the art of all possibilities when it comes to writing fiction and researching the paranormal is labor intensive indeed. For as many historical tales that are shared, there are equally as many ongoing in the present day and few are accurately recorded.

Stephen King, the great author of some of the most terrifying and highly successful best sellers, wrote a book that will forever impact my work. *On Writing: A Memoir of the Craft* (Pocket Books, 2000) played such a force in this work, its inspiration has carried me through the entire project as though King himself were sitting in front of me threatening to chop off a limb if I didn't trudge through properly. As a writing student in his printed and bound classroom, I learned boundaries regarding personal deadlines and descriptive banters from his thoughts and advice.

With *On Writing* as a guide, many of the facts that are embellished in these tales of terror can be attributed to some of the world's foremost authorities on the paranormal as well as some of Savannah's most distinguished writers and historians. Following is a bibliographical summary of my sources, all of which are highly recommended as further reading for those who are fans of the history of Savannah as well as the local horror genre.

BOOKS

Adams, James Mack. *Images of America: Tybee Island.* Charleston, SC: Arcadia
    Publishing, 2000.
This compilation of historic photographs and archival material from the Tybee Island Historical Society outlines the history (from the 1700s to present) of the mile-wide island that touches the mouth of the Savannah River. The book was used as a guide for describing an offshore ship sinking in chapter 12, "Shipwreck."

Debolt, Margaret Wayt. *Savannah Spectres and Other Strange Tales.* Atglen, PA: Schiffer Publishing, 1993–2008.

The psychic tales from local Savannahians, mixed with the late author's personal revelations and experiences, provide readers with a spiritual sampler of short stories that are lively and intriguing. Laying the groundwork for other authors playing on Savannah's psychic tales, this is a fun read from a lady who was the face of scary Savannah stories long before they were popular.

Dick, Susan E., and Mandi D. Johnson. *Images of America: Savannah: 1733 to 2000.* Charleston, SC: Arcadia Publishing, 2001.

Photographs displayed throughout this book were used to describe Savannah in the 1700 and 1800s as well as buildings that are still standing today. This resource provided authentic photographs of buildings as they appeared during that time period, and those photos assisted in the descriptions of the city from 1733 to 2000 that may be found in all chapters.

Dick, Susan E., Amie Marie Wilson, and Mandi Dale Johnson. *Images of America: Historic Bonaventure Cemetery: Photographs from the Collection of The Georgia Historical Society.* Charleston, SC: Arcadia Publishing, 1998.

The discovery of this 126-page publication was instrumental in providing aesthetic details in chapter 6, "Bonaventure: No Way Out," and chapter 7, "Gracie." It is an excellent source for those interested in touring historic Bonaventure Cemetery and contains both history and directions to the grave sites of prominent Savannahians buried there with specific section and lot numbers listed in detail.

Holzer, Hans. *The Phantoms of Dixie.* Indianapolis and New York: Bobbs-Merrill Company, 1972.

Holzer visits each Southern state and shares his version of terror in twelve chapters. His book was used to research the details of the hanging of the first woman in Savannah, whose spirit roams Wright Square in chapter 5, "The Wrongs of Wright Square."

Kingery, Dorothy Williams. *Savannah's Jim Williams & His Southern Houses.* Sheldon Group, L.L.C, 1999.

Dr. Kingery's tabletop book is a fascinating and well-written, comprehensive compilation filled with original photographs and documentation from her brother, James A. Williams's, fine restoration work in the Savannah. Sadly, Dr. Kingery passed away in early 2023. Her book is timeless.

Roberts, Nancy. *Georgia Ghosts.* Winston-Salem, NC: John F. Blair, 1997.
One of the South's greatest storytellers is Nancy Roberts, who has written more than twenty books on the supernatural. This is one of Roberts's great trips through the state of Georgia, revealing several stories from Savannah landmarks such as The Olde Pink House, the Hampton Lillibridge House, the 17Hundred90 Inn, and the Shrimp Factory, among others.

———. *Ghosts and Specters of the Old South.* Orangeburg, SC: Sandlapper Publishing, 1974.
Nancy Roberts's lively way of bringing the supernatural into the hearts of readers has earned her a special place in the lineage of authors on the paranormal. Her flair for entertaining the reader was an inspiration when *Haunted Savannah* was a mere notebook full of pencil-scratched ideas.

Roll, William G. *The Poltergeist.* New York: Paraview Special Editions, 2004. (Previously published by Doubleday, New York, in 1972.)
This is the place to start if you're intrigued by the paranormal. Dr. William G. Roll was once considered the foremost expert on the subject. As a frequent guest on television's *Unsolved Mysteries,* he has been seen on the Discovery Channel, and in 1996, he received the Outstanding Career Award from the Parapsychological Association. Dr. Roll headed up Duke University's Department of Parapsychology until he assumed his last professional role as a professor at Middle Georgia College. He was contacted by the late Jim Williams in the 1970s to visit and study activities in his home on St. Julian Street, the Hampton Lillibridge House. Although official results of that study were unattainable, Williams's opinions of Dr. Roll are expressed in various chapters throughout the book. My attempts to reach Dr. Roll were unsuccessful.

Savannah Department of Cemeteries. *The Historical Society Guide to Bonaventure Cemetery.*

This is a free brochure available at the entrance of Bonaventure Cemetery. It offers an accurate description of the grounds as well as a plat showing the sections and grave site numbers. The brochure goes hand-in-hand with the *Images of America: Historic Bonaventure Cemetery* book described earlier. It was used in describing locations for the grave sites of John Walz in chapter 6 and Gracie Watson in chapter 7.

Stavely, John F. *Ghosts and Gravestones of Savannah, Georgia.* Savannah, GA: Historic Tours of America, 2006.
It is always helpful to view Savannah's tales as other writers have recorded them. Stavely is not only a storyteller, but also an acclaimed performer. As the recent national director for Historic Entertainment for Historic Tours of America, Inc., he created Savannah's popular "Ghosts and Gravestones Tour." His notoriety has spread though appearances on the Discovery Channel, Travel Channel, History Channel, and Food Network. Recently he was featured on *Ghost Hunters, Most Haunted Places,* and *Great Hotels.* Although he is not a resident of Savannah, his tours have become one of the city's most adored attractions. His writings are short, factual recounts of what has been seen in and around downtown Savannah and were utilized for information only.

NEWSPAPERS, ARCHIVES, AND WEBSITES

"Alice R., Not Polly B., Hanged First in State." *Savannah Morning News,* date unknown.
This article contradicts the actual historical facts proven in earlier *(Savannah) Morning News* microfilm from the 1700s. It was shared in a column written by Porter Carswell titled "Georgia Folklore" and was used as research for chapter 5, "The Wrongs of Wright Square."

The Atlanta Journal and Constitution Magazine, September, 13, 1964.
This article is an interview with Jim Williams about his encounters with ghosts at The Hampton Lillibridge House in Savannah.

Coffey, Tom. "Add 'Miss Jane' to Our Ghosts." *Savannah Morning News,* November 29, 1981.

This article was used as direction in outlining the story "Miss Jane's Revenge," chapter 4. According to Coffey's column, the story was originally written by a member of the Charles Colcock Jones Jr. family and edited by Lilla Mills Hawes of the Georgia Historical Society. The original story was published in a brochure by the Georgia Historical Society in 1981, and a photocopy was obtained with permission at the Historical Society's Hodgson Hall. It was embellished and retold in my own words in this book with credit provided within the chapter.

"The Funeral of Miss Gordon." *(Savannah) Morning News,* December 30, 1880.
This article describes the upcoming funeral plans for Miss Sarah Alice Gordon, daughter of the ghost at the Juliette Gordon Low Birthplace. The article was used to authenticate the trials of Sarah Gordon, the ghost described in chapter 1, "No Rest for Sarah."

Gordon Family Papers. Georgia Historical Society, Savannah.
This is a collection of Gordon family materials, including personal handwritten letters, diaries, deeds, and memorabilia. Several items were utilized in capturing the personalities of members of the Gordon family in chapter 1 and chapter 2, "Willie and Nelly."

"Haunted Hotels in Georgia." thingsthatgoboo.com/hauntedplaces/haunted georgia.
This article outlines the unknown author's experiences in the 17Hundred90 Inn. It was used as a reference for chapter 21, "The Confessions of Anna."

Historical Marker Database. hmdb.org.
This is an excellent resource for reviewing historical markers in the state of Georgia without having to find each one.

Indiana Paranormal Society. "Findings from the Study of 17Hundred90 Inn, Savannah, GA, July 2010."
This article reviews the strange occurrences that were recorded during a study of the 17Hundred90 building. It was used as a basis for the story in chapter 21.

Mason, Lynelle S. *Lighthouse Digest* (online). September 9, 2003. Article, "Georgia's Cockspur Island Light, Home of the Waving Girl."
Used in chapter 3, "The Waving Girl."

McQuade, Jack. "Flags, Cuspidor, Dungeon, Found in Pulaski Wreckage." *Savannah Morning News,* January 29, 1957.
This article was used as research in writing chapter 8, "A Banker's Nightmare."

New Georgia Encyclopedia. georgiaencyclopedia.org.
This is an excellent resource for researching some of Georgia's most prominent citizens. It was referred to in several instances and for many chapters throughout this book.

Power, Cheryl Harris. theshrimpfactory.com/haunted.
The owner's account of the ghosts in the upstairs storage room at the popular Shrimp Factory restaurant was taken into consideration when writing chapter 18, "The Spirits of the Shrimp Factory."

"Sad Bereavement." *(Savannah) Morning News,* December 29, 1880.
This article describes the illness and telegram sent to the parents of Miss Sarah Alice Gordon, daughter of the ghost, Sarah, who appears at the Juliette Gordon Low Birthplace. Details were used in describing the great sadness the mother experienced in chapter 1.

"Sad Bereavement." *(Savannah) Morning News,* December 31, 1880.
This is the actual funeral announcement for Alice, the daughter of Captain W. W. Gordon. Her body was delayed in being transported by train from New York to Savannah for burial. It was used to authenticate the sadness experienced in the main character's life in chapter 1.

Weeks, Carl Solana. *Savannah in the Time of Peter Tondee: The Road to Revolution in Colonial Georgia.* Columbia, SC: Summerhouse Press, 1997.
This book is an excellent narrative focusing on the subject of Peter Tondee, who was a tavern keeper and Revolutionary War character. The book was used to research the baby born to the woman hanged in chapter 5.

YouTube.com. youtube.com.

This website proved to be entertaining and, in some cases, helpful in researching various ghosts throughout the book. Specifically, readers will find it intriguing to watch the actual police footage of the ghostly disappearance of the automobile written about in chapter 14, "Ghost Car." The direct link is youtube.com/watch?v=uPNhuz1em4A&feature=related, or visit YouTube and type in "Ghost Car, Garden City, GA."

APPENDIX B

SAVANNAH'S SPOOKY TOURS

Savannah's scary side is best experienced when it's dark and her secrets are illuminated by the moon! Bring your most comfy pair of walking shoes or, if you dare, climb aboard a trolley and brave the historic squares, old inns and restaurants, and maybe a few dark alleys with a professional tour guide.

The past will come alive in tales of pirates, tragedies, and ghostly encounters so bring your courage and dare to explore the hauntings of this city.

A constantly updated list of tour companies can be found on visitsavannah .com/list/savannah-ghost-tours.

CHAPTER 1, NO REST FOR SARAH, AND
CHAPTER 2, WILLIE AND NELLY

The Juliette Gordon Low Birthplace is open Monday, Tuesday, Thursday through Saturday, 10:00 a.m. to 4:00 p.m. The address is 10 East Oglethorpe. For more information, call (912) 233-4501 or visit juliettegordonlowbirthplace.org.

CHAPTER 3: THE WAVING GIRL

A life-size sculpture of Florence Martus stands at the southeast end of Savannah's River Street. The sculptor Felix de Weldon is credited with the likeness of Martus, her collie, a small lantern, and a waving flag. The statue is a present-day beacon and tribute to Miss Martus, who was the city's unofficial greeter of all vessels in and out of the Savannah port for forty-four years.

CHAPTER 4: MISS JANE'S REVENGE

The home in which Miss Jane and the Jones brothers lived is no longer standing. Miss Jane, however, continues to be seen dressed in her thin gown wandering

Wright Square at night. After years of mistreatment from a husband who escaped with her wealth, she finally came to peace thanks to the help of the Jones brothers. The story appearing in this book was retold utilizing some of the actual dialogue taken directly from the Georgia Historical Society's newsletter where the story first appeared. Written by the newsletter editor, Lilia M. Hawes, the original story, called "Jones Sees a Ghost," is available in a printed brochure at the Georgia Historical Society at 501 Whittaker Street (912-651-2125) or visit the website at georgiahistory.com.

Hawes included the following note in the brochure, preceding the story:
This little notebook with the story, in Jones' beautiful and distinctive handwriting, was given to the Georgia Historical Society along with some other family papers by Page Anderson Platt (Mrs. Henry Norris), grand-niece of Mrs. Henry R. Jackson, nee Florance Barclay King, daughter of Thomas Burler King, to whom C. C. Jones presented this copy in 1876.
—*Lilla M. Hawes, Editor*

CHAPTER 5: THE WRONGS OF WRIGHT SQUARE

Wright Square is a public square. Although it is open for viewing twenty-four hours a day, it is not advised to visit the squares after 10:00 p.m., and most especially alone. Visit the east side of the square, and you'll notice places in the treetops where moss will not grow due to the shedding of blood there long ago.

CHAPTER 6: BONAVENTURE: NO WAY OUT

Bonaventure Cemetery is on the National Register of Historic Places and is open to the public from 10:00 a.m. to dark. Visit bonaventurehistorical.org for more information. Caretakers have asked that visitors observe and respect the grounds, a working cemetery where services may be ongoing throughout the week. A footnote: Alcohol is not allowed on the premises.

CHAPTER 7: GRACIE

The statues that sculptor John Walz delivered to Savannah early in his career may be viewed at the Telfair Academy of Arts and Sciences, 121 Barnard Street. Call (912) 790-8800 or visit telfair.org for hours. Gracie Watson lived from 1883 to 1889. After a short bout of pneumonia, she was pronounced dead just two days after Easter in 1889. Her parents hosted a funeral in the parlors of the Pulaski House, which they managed. Gracie is buried in Section E, Lot 99, in Bonaventure Cemetery. Bonaventure Cemetery is located at 330 Bonaventure Road, Thunderbolt, GA (912-651-6843; savannahga.gov/cityweb/cemeteriesweb.nsf/cemeteries/bonaventure.html). Several Savannah tours include Bonaventure on their stops.

CHAPTER 8: A BANKER'S NIGHTMARE

Standing on the site of the Pulaski Hotel today is Region's Bank. Prior to the bank's occupation of that corner, Morrison's Cafeteria stood there and before that, the Piccadilly, another cafeteria. Early news reports confirm "strange happenings" occurring in the restaurants' basement and bathrooms. Employees working in the bank today deny that they have experienced any strange occurrences.

CHAPTER 9: THE OLDE PINK HOUSE

The Olde Pink House is located at 23 Abercorn Street. The restaurant serves lunch and dinner, and reservations are always recommended by calling (912) 232-4286. The restaurant is composed of several different delightful areas for dining: sidewalk tables (weather permitting), a connecting sports bar dining area, the tavern (below the restaurant and a more casual experience that is first-come, first-served only), and the main dining rooms. The ghost of James Habersham has been seen in several areas of the house, and the ghost seen by the manager, Blanche, was viewed and photographed in the tavern.

CHAPTER 10: BROUGHTON AND BULL

The restaurant was called Il Pasticcio when the mysterious banging was reported. Today it is under new ownership and houses a Savannah family jewelry store called Levy Jewelers. The site is located at 2 East Broughton Street (912-231-8888; broughtonandbull.com).

CHAPTER 11: THE SPIRITS OF GRAYSON STADIUM

Beautiful Grayson Stadium is located at 1401 East Victory Drive. The facility is home to The Savannah Bananas. Savannah's first professional baseball team began in 1904, and parts of the stadium were completed in 1941. Visit the website thesavannahbananas.com for a schedule and list of fun stadium activities. Tickets are for sale online and the team usually sells out long before the season starts.

CHAPTER 12: SHIPWRECK

As you enter Tybee Island via US Highway 80 East, stay on the main road, Butler Avenue. At the curve in the road stands the massive anchor described in this chapter. Several artifacts from the shipwrecked SS *Republic* have been displayed in museums, however, none of them locally. Litigation is still pending in multiple lawsuits disputing the ownership of the more than a third of the coins said to be on board and discovered in the wreckage found about a hundred miles offshore of Tybee. The coins found are said to be worth $75 million. Each spring, college students flock to Tybee Island. Few return to school with true suntans, but many have reported the ghostly spirit of a mother walking the strand, searching for her child, on a chilly, windy day.

CHAPTER 13: THE FITZROY SAVANNAH

Fitzroy's is a delightful place to enjoy a true Savannah experience with friendly waitstaff and talkative bartenders. The tiny pub is located at 9 Drayton Street and is open for dinner. Call (912) 210-5980 or visit thefitzroysavannah.com for more information. If you sit at the bar, look for the strange orbs that appear sporadically. From your table, you may catch a glimpse of old Bud "Brute" Bailey hanging from the area in the rear of the room. One never knows who might be lurking in Isaac's on any given day.

CHAPTER 14: GHOST CAR

Instant chills occur when watching the video of a Garden City police officer's chase involving a car that vanished on the outskirts of Savannah. Visit youtube .com, type in "Ghost Car, Garden City, GA," and explore the mystery firsthand, just as Officer Greg Jones did that fateful night in August. Don't be deceived. Although some claim the event actually occurred in Garden City, New York, that is false. And if you travel on I-95 in the area around I-16, keep your eyes open for a strange white car with the vapor of a driver.

CHAPTER 15: BURIED ALIVE

Colonial Park Cemetery is one of Savannah's most beautiful and interesting places to visit. Open from dawn until dusk, there are several famous Savannahians buried there, including Button Gwinnett, one of the signers of the Declaration of Independence. Additionally, during the yellow fever epidemic of 1820, more than seven hundred victims died and were buried there until there was no more room. If you come by carriage, be sure to meet the driver face-to-face. One such tour company is Carriage Tours of Savannah (912-236-6756; carriagetoursofsavannah.com).

CHAPTER 16: HAUNTINGS FROM THE HOSPITAL

The old Candler Hospital stands on East Huntingdon Street between Drayton and Abercorn. It is off-limits to visitors and now stands as Ruskin Hall, owned by the Savannah College of Art and Design. The historical marker for the building is intriguing and still reads as follows:

> *Warren A. Candler Hospital: Georgia's first hospital, this institution is believed to be the second oldest general hospital in continuous operation in the United States. It was founded in 1803 as a seamen's hospital and poor house and was incorporated in 1808 under the name of Savannah Poor House and Hospital Society. The hospital was removed to this site in 1819.*
> *In 1835 a new charter was obtained for the institution.*
> *During the War Between the States a portion of the Hospital was*

used for the care of Confederate soldiers. In the area to the rear a stockade was erected in 1864, around the great oak that still stands there, for confinement of Union prisoners.

After Sherman's occupation of Savannah and until 1866 the building served as a Union hospital.

The name was changed in 1872 to Savannah Hospital. From 1871 to 1888 the Savannah Medical College was located here.

In 1876 the building was completely renovated. However, the structure of the 1819 building was retained and remains as the nucleus of the present hospital. In 1931 the Methodist Church acquired the facilities, and the name changed to honor Bishop Warren A. Candler.

The marker is available for public viewing and is located on Huntingdon Street near Drayton Street.

CHAPTER 17: HABERSHAM HALL

Habersham Hall is owned by the Savannah College of Art and Design and is used as classroom space. Offered as a stop on many Savannah tours, it is not open to the public but may be viewed from street level.

CHAPTER 18: THE SPIRITS OF THE SHRIMP FACTORY

Reservations are always recommended at the Shrimp Factory, located at 313 East River Street (theshrimpfactory.com). The "call-in" procedure is unique: Dial (912) 236-4229 or e-mail contact@theshrimpfactory and leave your name, time of arrival, and number of guests in your party. Upon arrival, you'll get priority over guests who walk in.

CHAPTER 19: THE BRIDE OF FORSYTH PARK

Forsyth Park is open daily from dawn until dark. There is a walking trail around the entire park that is approximately one mile from start to finish. Each year around St. Patrick's Day, the fountain sprays green water to commemorate the holiday

and associated festivities. And every time a couple weds in front of the two-tiered cast-iron monument, there is always the risk of a shadow covering the face of the bride to tarnish the beauty of the special day. Since Ammie's wedding, however, there have been no further reports.

CHAPTER 20: 117 LINCOLN STREET

The Lincoln Street condo is a private residence. The condo can be viewed, however, from street level. The site, when facing the building, is the first balcony up to the left of the front door entrance. As a courtesy to the owners, please refrain from disrupting the peace of the residence. Some names in this story were changed.

CHAPTER 21: THE CONFESSIONS OF ANNA

The 17Hundred90 Inn is located at 307 East President Street. As an inn, restaurant, and tavern, it is a charming place to dine, stay, or explore. For more information, call (912) 236-7122 or visit 17Hundred90.com. The inn is a popular stop on any of the Savannah ghost tours, and there's a dummy of a woman peering out a window that depicts Anna.

CHAPTER 22: THE MOON RIVER BREWING COMPANY

The Moon River Brewing Company is open Monday through Thursday, 11:00 a.m. to 11:00 p.m.; Friday and Saturday, 11:00 a.m. to midnight; and Sunday, 11:00 a.m. to 11:00 p.m. The restaurant and bar is located at 21 West Bay Street. For more information, call (912) 447-0943 or visit moonriverbrewing.com.

CHAPTER 23: TYBEE'S 12TH TERRACE GHOST

Tybee Island has seen its share of monstrous disasters with a major hurricane in 1893 and many more, including tropical storms, that have left marks on the island's inhabitants. Those disasters leave many unsettled spirits roaming the streets and beaches in search of peaceful rest. Indeed, Tybee's reputation as a historic treasure along the Atlantic coast is filled with folly and haunts. Located just minutes from Savannah, the island boasts tales of ghostly beings who have taken up residence with the vacationers and full-timers who live and visit there today. There's a small street, 12th Terrace, located ideally between the city government offices and the hotel/town center district. Some homes have been restored, others, newly built. But there's one residence there that once belonged to a very prominent Savannahian who hosted her granddaughters every summer. The problem is, she continues admonishing the girls, especially when vacationing renters are enjoying staying in this classic beach house. Since the home is private, don't expect a tour. But always keep your ears open if you're nearby, for her gen-teel and haunting voice that will bring chills, even in the heat of summer. For more information, contact VisitTybee.com.

CHAPTER 24: THE HOUSE ON ST. JULIAN STREET

This classic home is resting peacefully at 507 East St. Julian Street near Wash-ington Square. Several downtown walking tours can lead you there by foot. Once you've arrived, respectfully gaze upon the New England-styled dwelling and real-ize one thing: although it has seen its share of fame, this home today, is not open for tours. It is private. Within its walls lies a host of ghostly beings, timeless horror stories and frightful events that started in 1796 when the home was originally built and then later moved through the streets of downtown Savannah. Combined with a host of onlookers, residents, workers and a revolving door of owners, there are few answers to the countless mysteries at this address. Brought to fame by Savannah's renowned preservationist Jim Williams, today, one might glance up to hear echoes of laughter and the clanging of glassware. This is indeed, "The most haunted house in Savannah," carrying on its tradition of ghostly (and dead) Savannahians, still partying to this day. For more information, visit Savannah His-tory and Haunts, a walking tour: https://www.savannahhistoryandhaunts.com.

ABOUT THE AUTHOR

Georgia Byrd, a travel writer by trade, was first spooked by Savannah's specters while chaperoning her son and nine of his friends on a walking ghost tour of Savannah in 1988. Standing on the corner of St. Julian Street, gazing upward and into the windows of the Hampton Lillibridge House, she first took the subject of ghosts lightly. But when the group scattered after viewing a tall man dressed in black peering through the third-story window, she became an instant believer.

Thrust into the evil lurking near her third-floor office in the centuries-old *Savannah Morning News* Building at 111 Bay Street, she became intrigued by the stories shared by a coworker and friend, Margaret Wayt Debolt (now deceased), who authored one of the first books on Savannah ghosts. Ironically, it was under Byrd's direction that Ms. Debolt wrote a series of articles for *Savannah Magazine* that led to her following up with a haunted book of her own.

Byrd, a former newspaper editor and columnist, was the founding editor of *Savannah Magazine,* and meeting deadlines took the spotlight away from ghosts in the city . . . at least for a while. Her work with *Savannah Magazine* in the 1990s, coupled with the help of exemplary photography by her husband, Joseph, led to more than fifty regional and national awards for editing, graphic design, content, and art direction.

When a business meeting at Savannah's First City Club exposed her to some of the management at *Forbes,* she was reminded of her childhood dream: to one day work for that magazine. Since that day in 1990, she has produced advertising supplements on yachting and economic development while calling Savannah and Charleston her home. In between sampling some of the world's largest mega-yachts firsthand in both calm and stormy seas, she has learned to cope with the paranormal in her own home and succeeded.

The author of *Insiders' Guide to Savannah and Hilton Head* (eighth edition, Globe Pequot Press), Byrd is also author of three editions of *Romantic Days & Nights in Savannah* (Globe Pequot Press), *The History of Aviation in Savannah* (Savannah Airport Commission), and coauthor of *Seasons of Savannah* (Savannah College of Art and Design) and *Megayachts of the World* (Edisea Ltd.). Following her deadline for this book, she recently added her flair for writing to *Haunted*

Charleston. She has appeared on the Travel Channel, CNN, *Good Morning America*, and *The Today Show* as a travel and yachting consultant. A contributor to *Atlanta Magazine*, *Southern Living*, and the *Atlanta Journal-Constitution*, among others, she continues to write from her office overlooking the salt marshes behind her island home, fully aware of the fact that at any time, some things that are strange, unusual, and truly unexplainable could disrupt her work.